I0779392

ELLEN FANNON

FALLING FOR A COWBOY

By Ellen Fannon

BOOK TWO IN THE LOVE IN THE WIND SERIES

ISBN-13: 978-1-962168-59-5

ALSO BY ELLEN FANNON

Other People's Children
Save the Date – 2022 Christian Indie Award winner
Don't Bite the Doctor
Honor Thy Father – Episode One
Honor Thy Father —Episode Two

LOVE IN THE WIND SERIES
Love in the Wind —Book One

Always a bridesmaid, *never a bride.* The unwelcome thought popped into Kendra Clark's head without warning as she pulled into the long driveway leading to Whispering Winds Ranch, one of the most beautiful places in southern Wyoming. Now where had *that* thought come from? Oh, she knew where. The last time she had been here she had been a bridesmaid in Ben and Darcy's wedding. Ben Parish, the owner of Whispering Winds had fallen hard for Darcy, the pretty new veterinarian who had moved to Wyoming to start a new life after her fiancé had dumped her a week before their wedding. Not so different from Kendra's own experience with her high school sweetheart, Aaron. Everyone, including them, expected them to get married, even though they had gone their separate ways to college with the understanding they would get married when they graduated. But the distance and time apart had pretty much killed their relationship. Well, that and the fact that apparently, Aaron hadn't considered remaining true to her during their four years apart a necessity. While she had been faithfully waiting for graduation when they could finally plan their wedding, he had been enjoying the company of numerous other coeds.

Although Kendra had been angry and disappointed, what bothered her most was the many opportunities she had passed up to date nice young men who had expressed an interest in her. Meanwhile, Aaron, too cowardly to admit the truth, had continued to lead her on, letting her think he was as anxious to start their life together as she was. Four wasted years later, he confessed he wasn't ready to settle down. By then, Kendra realized she had been more in love with the idea rather than the reality of Aaron. She'd never really known him at all.

Bittersweet memories of Ben and Darcy's fairy-tale-like wedding filled her mind as her tires crunched along the pebbled driveway. Not that she wasn't happy for them—she was. But it seemed like everyone in her singles' Sunday school class had paired up, leaving her the odd man out. Or, to be more accurate, the odd woman out. At the rate things were going, at the ripe old age of thirty-two, she'd be the only one left in the singles' class at church. Maybe she should promote herself to the old ladies' class. She felt more and more like an old maid as she watched all her friends get married while she seemed destined to be a single-for-lifer.

Kendra chided herself for her silliness. She certainly didn't need a man to complete or fulfill her life. As the youngest tenured professor at Blalock College, she had accomplished more than enough to lead a perfectly full and satisfying life. Maybe God intended for her to stay single. Besides, it wasn't as if she was actively looking for male companionship. She'd had opportunities for dates. But the pickings were somewhat slim in this small town. She'd dated a few men; other invitations she politely declined due to a complete lack of interest on her part. But nobody had ignited sparks. Was she too choosy? Perhaps. But deep down, she wanted her pulse to race and her insides to flutter when she thought of her true love, whoever he might be. Or maybe she was mixing up her expectations with a bad case of a stomach virus. The symptoms were fairly similar, other than one left you feeling euphoric, while the other left you wishing you were dead. Come to think of it, true love could leave a person wishing she were dead, too. But was it too much to ask for ooey-gooey, happily-ever-after love like in romance novels? Or in Ben and Darcy's relationship, which seemed as idyllic as any love story?

Get a grip on yourself, Kendra. The sensible voice in her head tried to rein in the ridiculous feelings that had come over her simply from entering a driveway, at the end of which sat the nearly hundred-year-old ranch house built by Ben's grandfather, where Ben and Darcy lived happily ever after. Kendra needed her brain to focus on the myriad of practical items on her to-do list—first and foremost of which was getting through the reception tonight for her graduate students.

She pulled her car up to the side of the house and turned off the engine, half-expecting to see Darcy come out to meet her. When no one appeared, Kendra exited the car and looked around, finally walking up to the back door.

Hmm, that's funny. The back door always stood open. She knocked and waited. Nothing. Frowning, she backed away from the door and picked her way carefully toward the barn, which sat a good hundred yards away from the house. Maybe they were cleaning out the stalls of the dozen or so horses that grazed in the spacious paddock just outside the barn.

Kendra's expensive heels didn't exactly do well on this turf as they sank into the soft, moist dirt. If she'd only known she would be tramping across this unlevel, unpaved ground, she would have changed clothes before heading straight out in her professional attire. But she had been in a hurry and hadn't counted on having to traipse to the barn. She stopped to pat the noses of a few curious horses who had wandered over to the fence to investigate the visitor. Although more comfortable around the animals than she had been a short while ago, she still felt a little overwhelmed by their size and strength. When she neared the door to the barn, the soft nickering of another horse, accompanied by a low, male voice, reached her ears.

"Ben?" she called out, as she stepped inside, kicking mud from her spiked heels.

A man standing with his back to her startled, knocking off a mug of coffee that had been resting on stacked hay bales next to where he had been placing a bridle on a horse. He jumped back as the black liquid landed in the straw at his feet, splashing over his boots and splattering his jeans. He turned, flinging coffee from his hand and wiping his hand on his pants. The horse he had been saddling up jerked back in surprise, as well.

It wasn't Ben. A man she had never seen before at the ranch stood glaring at her with intense dark eyes.

Kendra's hand flew to her mouth. "Oh, I'm so

sorry. I didn't mean to surprise you."

"Who are you?" he asked gruffly.

She took a tentative step toward him. "I'm Kendra Clark. I'm a friend of Ben and Darcy's." She debated briefly, then extended a hand.

He stared at her for a moment, then, with one corner of his mouth turning down, said, "I'd shake your hand, but I have hot coffee all over mine."

Kendra's eyes widened. "Oh, I'm so sorry," she repeated. "Did you get burned?"

He bent to retrieve the mug and mumbled, "I'll live." He walked past her out of the barn, forcing her to trot after him, trying not to get her heels stuck in the mud again. Setting his mug in the outdoor sink, he muttered, "Couldn't find my thermos. I knew I shouldn't have brought a mug out to the barn. Serves me right." With his back still facing her, he ran water over his hand and said, "Ben and Darcy aren't here."

"What time do you expect them back?" Kendra said, looking at her watch.

The man dried his hands on an old towel hanging from a nail above the sink. "A couple of days."

"*Days*?" Darcy had specifically told Kendra she could come by and borrow her punch bowl for the reception tonight. Had Darcy told her she would be going out of town? Kendra couldn't recall Darcy mentioning it. Still, it was Kendra's fault for leaving everything until the last minute. She should have picked up the punch bowl earlier in the week.

The man turned and leaned against the sink, scrutinizing her with an uncomfortable glower. "Yeah. They had a chance to take off for a couple of days. They didn't have a honeymoon."

Kendra nodded and bit her lower lip. She knew there hadn't been an opportunity for a honeymoon. Ben and Darcy deserved whatever little time they could steal away together. Kendra only wished they had let her know. But, in Darcy's defense, she probably thought Kendra had found another bowl somewhere else since Kendra hadn't gotten back to her. Now where was Kendra supposed to get a punch bowl at this late hour?

"So, what did you want?" The man's brusque tone jolted Kendra out of her churning thoughts.

"I don't suppose you know where Ben and Darcy keep their punch bowl, do you?" Kendra's brows raised in expectant hope.

He peered at her like she had suddenly sprouted horns from her head.

Kendra ducked her chin and pushed out a cheerless laugh. "No, of course you don't. Silly question." She turned to go. "I'm sorry to have bothered—"

"Can't say as I do." The man blew out a long breath. "But you can come in and look for it if you want." He readjusted his Stetson on his head and gestured for her to precede him to the house.

She stopped in her tracks, her mouth forming an "O." Then the tips of her lips curled up into a grateful smile. "Thanks. I would appreciate that."

Kendra felt his eyes on her as she tottered across the rough ground in her unsuitable shoes. She stopped at the back door and waited while he produced a key and unlocked the door. Then he motioned for her to enter, as he followed.

Kendra stopped in the middle of the huge kitchen. She loved this room with its wide plank floors, high arched ceiling letting in natural light through twin skylights, and the woodsy smell of pine. It put her spartan little kitchen to shame. But what she didn't love right now, as she stood gazing around, was the endless number of cupboards. Where should she start? She turned to the man who had stopped just inside the door, waiting with his hands on his hips. He obviously wasn't going to help, so she started opening one oak cabinet after another. Feeling somewhat like a guilty intruder going through her friends' personal space, she filled the uncomfortable silence in the room with endless chatter as she searched.

"I shouldn't have left this to the last minute, but I had so many other things to do," she said as she bent to peruse the contents of the cabinet next to the sink. "I wish I hadn't been put in charge of this reception. Things like this always make me so nervous. I'm afraid I'll forget something important." She straightened up and reached for the cabinet above her head. "But I guess since the reception is for my graduate students, it only makes sense for me to host it." She huffed out a self-conscious laugh. "Still, wouldn't you think a reception would fall under the job description of a secretary or something?"

He didn't reply, which only made her more nervous, and her words came out faster. "Not that I think the job is beneath me or anything like that, and it isn't as if my secretary hasn't helped. She's been wonderful. I just didn't want to ask her to take on more responsibility." Kendra slammed the cabinet door louder than she'd intended as she moved to the next one. "It's just that I've never had to organize something like this before. I don't know why I'm so worried about something so unimportant in the big scheme of things.

Not that a reception for my graduate students is unimportant, I didn't mean to imply that. They deserve recognition. They've worked hard."

Having exhausted all the cabinets within reach, she looked around and spied a step stool sitting against the wall. His eyes followed her as she pulled it next to the sink to access the upper cabinets. Again, although not looking at him, she could feel his eyes on her as she gingerly climbed onto the first step, trying to keep her tight skirt from riding up too high. Heat rose in her face, and she knew it accentuated her pale complexion. Why hadn't she taken the time to change clothes? Well, it was perfectly reasonable why she hadn't changed before coming here. She hadn't expected to be teetering on a step ladder in her professional attire. But she wished the taciturn man standing unhelpfully by the door wouldn't make her feel so uneasy.

Kendra raised another tentative leg, hiking her tight skirt slightly above her knee to bend it, and climbed onto the second step. She probably should have kicked off her shoes before attempting this ill-advised maneuver. She rummaged around in the top cabinet. "Nope, don't see it in here, either." She turned and partially faced him. "Oh, I guess I didn't tell you. I'm a professor of biology at Blalock." Now why had she felt the need to tell him that little piece of information? He certainly could care less. She rattled on. "I have three graduate students who are finishing their master's degrees. That's why I'm giving this reception. Well, it wasn't my idea," she continued, as she stretched to examine the cabinet next to the one she'd just inspected. "The dean suggested it would be a good idea and . . . Oh! I think I see it."

She went up on tiptoe while trying to kick her other leg out for balance. Her arm strained to grasp the edge of the bowl. The fleeting thought went through her head that she would have been better off to climb down and move the ladder over, but she was so close. Just as her fingers brushed the bowl, her foot slipped. As if in slow motion, she felt her body tumbling, landing against something firm and solid.

The air rushed out of Ricky's lungs as he hit square on his back against the hardwood floor. His arms encircled the woman he'd just caught in midair, as she sprawled against his chest, restricting movement of his ribs. Her curly red hair tickled his nose, and before he reached up a hand to move it away from his face, he caught a faint whiff of something flowery on her neck. After a moment of stunned silence, the woman rolled off him and rested on her heels by his side.

Ricky struggled to draw in a breath.

"Are you okay?" she finally asked. "I'm so sorry. I'm such a klutz."

How many times was this woman going to injure him and apologize? He coughed and fought to sit up, ignoring her offered hand of help. Was anything broken? He didn't think so, as he forced himself to move his arms and legs. A dull ache pounded in his upper back muscles. Anger rose in his chest at her foolishness.

"What a crazy, stupid thing to do!" he snapped. "What were you thinking?"

Her eyes went wide, and her blanched face reddened. Then, to his dismay, tears welled up in her green eyes. *No, don't cry. Do* not *cry.* He couldn't handle a weeping female.

"I'm sorry," she blubbered. "I thought I could reach the bowl. Are you hurt?"

He ignored her question. He was getting tired of her saying she was sorry. "Why didn't you ask for help?" he said, his tone only slightly softer than a minute ago.

Her nostrils flared. "Why didn't you *offer* to help? You just stood there." She swiped a hand across her damp eyes before the tears could escape. The fire in her green eyes evidenced that the waterworks had stopped as suddenly as they had started. Thank goodness for a short flood.

"You're more than capable of asking for help. God knows you can speak. You jabbered enough about everything else." He held her furious gaze while running a hand through his disheveled hair and patting the floor behind him for his hat. "I figured you were one of those liberated women who has to do everything themselves. You seemed determined to do so."

She glared at him. "And I thought you might be a chivalrous man. I was obviously wrong." She adjusted her blouse and made an awkward attempt to get to her feet, then looked around for her shoes that had flown off in the fall.

He grunted and stood, one hand rubbing a kink in his back. "Would you like me to get the punch bowl for you?" His words came out more like a challenge than an offer.

She snatched a shoe off the floor and jammed it onto her foot. "Please!" she snapped.

Ricky righted the toppled step ladder and climbed up to retrieve the miserable object of her desire that had caused such an uproar. All this commotion over a stupid punch bowl. He thrust it at her, none too gently.

"Thank you," she said, although her tone didn't convey gratitude. She stomped through the door and out to her car without looking back. Her attempt at righteous indignation might have been humorous as she tromped out in those ridiculous spiked heels, but his back and shoulder throbbed too much from having been slammed to the floor to be amused.

He waited until she started up her car and zoomed down the driveway spewing dust and gravel. Then, shaking his head, he exited the kitchen, locked the back door, and stood for a moment watching her car disappear along the road.

She was an egghead. Figured. A college professor, no less. Why were the intellectuals always the most clueless? They never had common sense. Fretting about some absurd reception, like it mattered one way or the other. He blew out a disgusted breath. He had real work to get back to.

CHAPTER TWO

Kendra drove away much too fast, her jaw clenching and her heart pounding. Not only had the rude cowboy insulted and humiliated her, but he had been oblivious to the fact she needed a little help. No, he hadn't been oblivious—he could plainly see she needed help. He had been arrogant and impertinent. All he had to do was *say* something instead of standing by the door like a silent guard who couldn't leave his post. Any other man would have rushed to relieve her of the step ladder and gotten the bowl for her instead of waiting until she fell and almost broke her neck. It should have been intuitively obvious to the oaf that she was not dressed for scaling ladders. Yet he did nothing.

Her angry brain composed a scenario of reporting the man's boorish behavior to Ben and Darcy when they returned. But as she wrestled with the words, they sounded foolish in her mind. How much more so would they sound to her friends? The man's job description certainly didn't include catching silly women when they fell off step stools they had no business being on in the first place wearing tight skirts and heels. She rotated her shoulders, not sure if she had twisted something or if the tension of the last few minutes had them tied up in knots.

Drawing in a long breath, Kendra counted to ten as she blew it out slowly through her lips. Despite the discourteous treatment from Ben's ranch hand, she had a reception to prepare for. Continuing to rehash the incident would do nothing to put her in the proper frame of mind for the celebration tonight. She didn't want to start off the evening uptight and upset. So what if she had an unpleasant encounter with a hired ranch hand? Who cared what he thought about her? She'd likely never see him again, and neither one of them was hurt, so what did it matter? Trying to refocus, she pushed the incident to the back of her mind.

Two hours later, after a hot shower and a change of clothes, Kendra felt better. She headed back to the campus to finish setting up for the reception.

"Ricky told us you barely escaped a potential disaster," said Darcy before church on Sunday.

Kendra's lips compressed into a thin line. So much for not making an issue out of the episode she'd tried to forget. Feigning nonchalance, she replied, "It wasn't anything, really."

"That's not what Ricky said. You could have been seriously hurt falling off that step stool." Concern filled Darcy's eyes.

"Honestly, it was no big deal. I was foolish and . . ." Kendra had to grudgingly admit if the surly cowboy, whose name she now knew was Ricky, hadn't broken her fall, she could have been injured. Lowering her eyes, she muttered, "I guess I was fortunate he was there."

"I'm sorry I forgot about the punch bowl. I meant to set it out before we left." A mischievous grin lit up Darcy's face. "The opportunity to get away for a couple of days just came up, and we took it. I guess I was kind of in a hurry."

Kendra smiled. "It's okay. I hope you had a good time."

"We did." Darcy's cheeks reddened.

Kendra laughed. "Don't worry, I won't ask for details. I'll get the punch bowl back to you this week. That is if you're going to be around." No way did she want to run into the cowboy again.

"There's no hurry. I don't plan on using it anytime soon." Darcy touched Kendra's arm. "I'm just glad you're all right."

Kendra rolled her eyes. "Nothing hurt but my pride." Then she supposed she should make sure Ricky wasn't hurt. After all, he had taken the brunt of her fall. "And Ricky? Is he okay?"

Darcy laughed. "He's fine. He's a tough guy. Breaking your fall is nothing compared to wrangling cattle all day."

Kendra should have let the conversation drop. But for some reason, she felt compelled to continue. "Is Ricky always so . . . ." She searched for the right word to describe the man who made it clear he had no use for her.

Darcy nodded. "Ricky's the strong, silent type. But he's a good man. Trustworthy. And a great worker. Ben always puts him in charge when he's away."

Kendra huffed. He might be strong, but he sure wasn't silent when he'd berated her and made her feel beneath contempt.

"Don't let his tough exterior fool you. Underneath his hard, outer shell, he's a sweet, sensitive man."

Really? Kendra found that hard to believe. But who cared? Although Darcy's glowing assessment of the cowboy was admirable, it was unnecessary. Kendra doubted she'd ever see him again. In fact, with any luck, she wouldn't.

Kendra ran into him, literally, again the following Wednesday afternoon. She had a week off before the summer session started and planned to do some minor home improvements. Randal's Hardware in town carried a small selection of paint, and she hoped to find what she wanted without having to drive into Jackson Hole. Perusing the available options, she discovered that Mr. Randal could mix virtually any color she desired. She settled on a shade of light blue called dewdrop, unable to fathom who thought up the designations for paint hues. Someone with a lot more time and imagination than she had. Regardless of the name, the color should go nicely in her guest bedroom, which, to be honest, hadn't had guests since her parents had visited two years ago. Still, the room needed a touch-up.

With her mind on the painting project she wanted to finish this week, she didn't watch where she was going as she hurried out of the hardware store with her can of dewdrop blue paint. She pushed against the glass door in her haste, shoving it into the man trying to enter.

The door smacked into his head, knocking his hat to the ground. He winced, and his hand flew to the reddened mark on his forehead as he bent to retrieve his hat.

"Oh, my goodness! I'm so sorry." Kendra set her paint can on the sidewalk and stooped at the same time to pick up the hat. As they both straightened up, the top of her head caught his chin.

He staggered back a step, then his eyes landed on her. "You!"

An involuntary gasp slipped through her lips. Her eyes grew large as a sense of horror washed over her. Surely this couldn't be happening again. Her voice got stuck in her throat.

His eyes locked onto hers for a long moment. Then he shook his head as a thin smile turned up the corners of his mouth. "Do you always cause this much destruction wherever you go?"

She winced. "Not usually. I don't suppose saying I'm sorry again would suffice."

His semi-smile threw her off. Was he going to yell at her once more for her carelessness, or did he suddenly find the whole situation amusing?

He settled the hat back on his head, his eyes turning serious. "May I ask you a question?"

Fearing the worst, she nodded, as her palms broke into a sweat.

"Do you shop here often?"

Her brows drew together in confusion. "No, why?"

The right side of his face curled up in a lop-sided grin, revealing a gorgeous dimple on his cheek. "Because I come here at least once a week. I was thinking that if you were also a frequent patron of this establishment, maybe we should work out a schedule. You know, so we don't keep running into each other, so to speak."

His eloquent speech rattled her. What kind of cowboy used words like "patron of this establishment?" Against her will, she allowed herself to relax. He was making a joke. Who would have figured? She reached up and brushed an errant curl from her face, feeling warmth creeping up her neck. What a curse to be a redhead. With her pale complexion, blushes were difficult to conceal.

Taking his cue at levity, she said, "You'll be happy to know I rarely patronize this establishment. So, you should be safe from Cyclone Kendra."

Merriment danced in his eyes. "That's good to know."

"Is your head—"

"Fine. I have a hard head. Or so I'm told."

She grinned. "You may find this hard to believe, but I generally don't go around injuring people wherever I go."

He raised his eyebrows. "So, it's just me? Should I be flattered or concerned?"

Kendra laughed. Just then, another customer walked out of the store and stumbled over the paint can she had left on the sidewalk.

"Oh! I'm sorry," she said, rushing to pick up the offending object.

The man shot her an annoyed look before continuing on his way.

Ricky chuckled. "Oh good. It's not just me."

She sighed. What was it about this man that made her so clumsy? Ordinarily, she was a graceful person. But each encounter with him—okay, all two of them— brought out the worst in her. He must think her completely incompetent. But she found herself drawn to his laughter, a genuine, happy sound. She certainly hadn't seen that side of him the other day. He had been aloof and cold.

"Sorry," he said, "I shouldn't be making fun of you."

"It's all right. I suppose I deserve it." She guessed it wouldn't do any good to repeat that she generally wasn't such a klutz. He would think she protested too much. Didn't he have business in the hardware store? Why was he still standing here making her feel like a bungling dimwit?

His eyes traveled to the can of blue paint she held. "Doing some painting?"

A change in subject. Thank goodness. "Yes. I'm off this week and doing some work around the house."

"I hope you don't paint like you do everything else. You may end up looking like a Smurf."

She flattened her lips. "Very funny. I'll have you know I'm a good painter. Besides, this is not Smurf color."

"Nevertheless, I recommend covering everything with a large tarp, including yourself. Have fun painting." He gave one more chuckle, then proceeded into the store.

Kendra stood staring after him, one hand holding the paint, the other on her hip. She wasn't sure whether to be irritated or amused. Whatever. He was an odd duck—one day dark and explosive, the next poking fun at her. Part of her wanted to dump the can of paint over his head. Another part of her wanted to run her hand gently over his forehead where she had slammed the door into it to make sure he didn't have a big goose egg. Gracious! Where had *that* thought come from?

Although good-looking, in a rugged, primitive sort of way, Ricky certainly wasn't the type of man she would ever be attracted to.

CHAPTER THREE

Ricky walked into the hardware store still chuckling. There was something about that redhead that tickled him, not the least of which was her complete lack of awareness of her surroundings and the ensuing, unintended, disastrous consequences she left in her wake. He could just picture her painting project, with half the paint on the wall and half on her, and for some reason, he found that image appealing. Surprised at himself, he stopped to consider why he even entertained such a thought.

Was he attracted to her? Gracious no! Women hadn't held any attraction for him since he lost Lily. That part of his life had died long ago, and he didn't care to resurrect it. Sure, the redhead was reasonably nice-looking as far as redheads went. He had never been particularly drawn to redheads, generally finding blondes more eye-catching. But those green eyes of hers, especially when they shimmered with tears, had sparkled like emeralds. He had never seen such an intense shade of green eyes before, and he had to admit they were striking. Still, even if he were the least bit attracted to her, which he wasn't, he would never become involved with an academic sophisticate. Give him the simple, uncomplicated life any day over highbrow society.

She was probably like all the others of her kind—good in her field and useless in everything else, yet always looking down on people who weren't on her intellectual level. He knew the type. They surrounded themselves with other lofty-minded individuals just like themselves, burying themselves in their ivory towers where real life couldn't reach them. Nope, no way could he ever become interested in a woman like that. So why did he keep thinking about her?

Darcy had told him Kendra went to church with her and Ben. Besides being an egghead, she was also religious. A strange combination. But if there was anything he disliked more than intellectuals, it was religious people. He knew Ben and Darcy were strong Christians, and he respected their beliefs, as long as they didn't try to push them on him. They had thrown out subtle hints, but Ricky put up his protective barriers against them. He had no use for God, either. God hadn't been there when he needed Him the most, so why should he serve a god like that? What was the point?

What had started him down this trail of thoughts? He was unlikely to run into the redhead again, and even if he did, so what? He felt his lips shift upward. If he ran into her again, she'd probably cause more physical pain to him. Forcing his mouth into a stern line, he recommitted what he'd determined years ago in his heart. Nobody was going to get close to him ever again.

Drat! Paint splattered from Kendra's roller, peppering her arm, T-shirt sleeve, and face with blue polka dots. She had obviously put too much paint on the roller. What was the matter with her? She could usually paint a room without so much as an errant drop of paint. Pursing her lips, she grabbed a rag and wiped her face and arm. It was that cowboy. He had jinxed her. His very presence made her a bumbling lummox. But that was ridiculous. He wasn't standing there watching her paint, thank goodness. Still, just the thought of him made her klutzy. She needed to rid herself of the image of his face with that yummy dimple on his right cheek as he teased her. Cute as he may be, he was not the type of man she would ever fall for.

She carefully wiped the excess paint from the roller against the side of the pan and attempted to refocus her mind on the job at hand. But she couldn't seem to get her thoughts off Ricky. How had he gone from rude and dismissive to almost flirty? No, no, not flirty. The man was probably well aware of his charms and used them on every woman. She would not be taken in by them. So why did the warning bell to watch out even go through her mind?

Vigorously maneuvering the roller over the boring white wall, Kendra tried to figure out how she had suddenly changed from a competent career woman to behaving like a gawky teenager. It had started with her feeling of being left behind as all her friends and acquaintances paired up. Then she encountered the cowboy who had reinforced her insecurities by making her feel careless. Sure, she should have asked for help in getting the bowl from the cabinet, but she was used to having to do things for herself. As he had so astutely pointed out, she *was* one of those independent women who was used to doing everything themselves. But, in her defense, she didn't have the luxury of a man at her fingertips to do her bidding. Plus, in all her thirty-two years, she had never fallen from a ladder. She just had the misfortune of doing so and humiliating herself in front of an unintended audience. But contrary to what Ricky thought of her, she was not a completely helpless woman. Good grief, she never would have gotten where she was if she were.

Then, just as she seemed to be getting back to normal, she'd literally run into him again today, only confirming his opinion of her as a hopeless klutz. But why did his opinion matter? She didn't need to impress him. After all, she held a master's and PhD degrees. He had probably not even graduated from high school. They were hardly in the same league. What could they possibly have in common?

Oh, dear! That sounded terribly snobbish, even in her private thoughts. Kendra rebuked herself. She had never been a prideful person, and now she had mentally dismissed another human being as being inferior because of educational differences. Shame burned within her.

The phone rang, and she clutched it from the table, grateful for an interruption to her unrestrained thoughts.

"Hello?" She glanced down at her hand holding the phone, noted smeared blue paint, and frowned.

"Kendra? It's Darin Frazier."

Darin Frazier? The new professor of biochemistry? The dreamy man whose appearance on campus had caused a massive release of estrogen from all female faculty and students alike? Why was he calling *her*? And how did he get her number?

"Kendra, are you there?"

She cleared her throat. "Uh . . . yes, sorry."

"Did I catch you at a bad time?"

Kendra's eyes traveled over her paint-covered shirt. "No, no, not at all." She perched against the edge of the table, trying to regain her composure after being stunned by Darin's unexpected phone call.

His smooth voice hummed in her ear. "I hope you don't mind my wheedling your number from the department secretary."

Oh, so he'd used his charm on Mrs. Levy, the white-haired grandmother who'd worked at the college forever. "No, of course not." *Why are you calling me?*

"Good, I'd hate to get the dear lady in trouble."

She wished Darin would get to the point and stop leaving her in suspense. After a pause, she said, "What can I do for you, Darin?"

"I suppose you heard about the faculty meeting that just came up for tomorrow afternoon."

Kendra stifled a groan. She had looked forward to this week off with no responsibilities at the college. "No, I didn't." She quickly thumbed through her phone and found an unread text. "Oh, I see it. I've been busy painting my guest room and haven't checked my messages."

A delightful laugh came from the other end of the phone. "You sound as thrilled as I am."

She joined him with a little laugh. "Well, you know faculty meetings. The bane of professors' existence."

"So true. But a necessary evil, nonetheless."

"Well, I thank you for letting me know—"

"That's not the only reason I called."

She suddenly realized she would have gotten the

message without Darin's informing her. "Oh?"

"I thought that after we've suffered through the tedium of a faculty meeting, you might care to join me for dinner at La Traviata. We'll have earned a reward."

La Traviata? The most expensive restaurant within a thirty-mile radius? Kendra's heart skipped a beat. Was he asking her on a date? Well, of course he was asking her on a date. People didn't just casually drop in at La Traviata like it was the neighborhood pizza joint.

A delighted laugh escaped her lips. "I would love to." She didn't admit that she had lived here for over twenty years and had never eaten at La Traviata. He would think her an unsophisticated bumpkin.

"Wonderful. I'll make reservations for seven. I look forward to seeing you tomorrow."

"Yes, I'll see you tomorrow." Kendra pushed the end call button and gave a whoop of giddy joy. Clapping her hands together, she danced across the room. "I have a date with Professor Dreamy! *Me*! He asked *me*!" All the other women at the school would be green with envy.

Her black cat, Seymour, wandered into the room, apparently interested in what his mistress was so excited about. Normally, she would shoo him away from the paint, but today, she swept him into her arms, ignoring her blue hands. "Can you believe it, Seymour?"

The cat let out an irritated yowl and fidgeted to be let loose, sashaying out the room with an arrogant swish of his tail which now sported a blue splotch at the end.

"Fine. Don't be happy for me," she called after him. She turned to pick up her roller as the image of Ricky flashed into her mind. Whoa! What was *that* all about? Kendra shook her head to dislodge the image and went back to work.

26

CHAPTER FOUR

"Wow, where'd you get that goose egg?" asked Ben, as Ricky pulled off his hat and wiped the sweat from his brow with the back of his gloved hand. A sluggish breeze did little to alleviate the heat, only managing to stir up a cloud of dust under their feet.

They were finishing up for the afternoon, unsaddling their horses after riding through the ranch checking the herd of Angus cattle grazing on the hill. Thankfully, no animal in the group appeared to be ill or injured, and the men could enjoy another peaceful evening with no crisis to attend to.

Ricky touched the knot on his head that he had forgotten about until the rough swipe with his glove reminded him of its presence.

"Is it that bad, boss?"

Ben squinted at him. "It's a nice shade of purple, which isn't your color."

"Your crazy redhead beaned me with the door at the hardware store. Good for me my head was turned to the side or she'd have probably broken my nose."

"My crazy redhead?" Ben raised one eyebrow.

"Yeah, you know. Candy, Kendy, something-or-other." Ricky darn well knew her name, but for some reason, he didn't want to let Ben know he knew.

Ben scratched his head. "You mean Kendra?"

Ricky feigned ignorance. "Yeah, I think that's her name." He busied himself with untacking his horse so he didn't have to look Ben in the eye.

"Did you put some ice on it?"

"Nah, I'm okay."

"What was Kendra doing at the hardware store?" Ben pulled the saddle off his favorite horse, Malachi, and stood waiting for Ricky.

The tips of Ricky's ears flamed. "How should I know? All I know is she was in a hurry and rammed into me without looking where she was going. That woman is like a bull in a china shop."

Ben shot him a curious look. "First she literally falls into your arms"—he stopped, a smirk playing about his lips—"then she bangs into you with a door. Sounds like the lady is trying to get your attention."

Ricky scowled at him. "Just keep her away from me, okay? Next time she's likely to kill me." He grabbed his saddle and strode quickly to the barn, leaving Ben behind. He didn't want to talk about Kendra with Ben. Or with anyone else, for that matter. And he didn't like the smirk on Ben's face. Plus, his head now throbbed, thanks to Ben for calling it to his attention.

Ben followed him, apparently determined not to let the conversation go. "You could do a lot worse than Kendra," he said, grabbing a rag from a peg on the wall to wipe down his saddle.

"Who says I'm looking?" Ricky avoided Ben's insistent gaze.

"Nobody. It's just that you're single, she's single—"

Ricky snorted. "Well, that about sums up the extent of our compatibility. Besides, I don't like redheads."

Ben stopped his work and pinned Ricky with a stare he couldn't ignore. "Seems to me you don't like blondes or brunettes either. I've never seen you with a woman."

Ricky's jaw tightened. "Look, boss, just 'cause you got bit by the love bug doesn't mean the rest of us have to follow your lead. Maybe I'm happy being a bachelor. Don't start trying to play matchmaker. Seems to me that up until a few months ago, you were in the same boat."

Ben nodded and rubbed a hand over his face. "Yeah, you're right. But I didn't know what I was missing."

Ricky settled his saddle on the rack and turned to face his boss. "Look, if I need help with you setting me up with someone, how about I let you know?"

"Fair enough. I won't bring it up again." Ben resumed wiping down his saddle. "But for the record, Kendra is not *my* redhead. I happen to be happily married to a gorgeous brunette."

Ricky hung up the rest of his tack and said, "I'm gonna head home if that's all for today."

"Yeah, sure. See you tomorrow." Ben waved his hand in dismissal.

Ricky tromped to his Ranger pickup, irritation gnawing at his gut. He didn't like people getting into his personal business. Ben was a great boss and they worked well together, but Ricky hadn't moved to Wyoming to make friends. He'd come to escape the noise and stress of life in the fast lane and lose himself in the beauty and simplicity of ranching—not to mention outrunning his demons. He hadn't told anyone his history, nor did he intend to. So far, he'd managed to keep his distance. No one was ever going to get close to him again. And the last thing he needed was a woman to complicate his life. Especially *that* one.

He started the engine and pulled out down the long driveway, his thoughts taking over his mind. As if *that* woman had the least desire to complicate his life. They hardly ran in the same circles. She probably regarded him as a working peon, clearly beneath her lofty academic status. He smiled to himself. If she only knew. Then the smile slipped from his face. She would never know.

CHAPTER FIVE

Kendra felt like a fidgety child as she willed the boring faculty meeting to wrap up. The hum of the air-conditioner and the monotoned voice of Dr. Cochran threatened to lull her to sleep, and she fought to stay awake. Across the table, Darin caught her eye and sneaked a wink. Her pulse quickened and she stifled a giggle. Instantly alert, she could just imagine what the other members of this stodgy group would think about two of their esteemed colleagues flirting like teenagers during the conduction of this serious business. Serious business, hah! More bloviating about budgets and other dull details to which she would just as soon not be privy. Most of these mandatory meetings had little to do with her day-to-day duties. Under the table, her leg jiggled with nervous energy. Would Dr. Cochran, the pompous windbag who was speaking, *ever* get to the point and finish? Or did he just love the sound of his own voice? Kendra tuned him out, as she anticipated the evening ahead.

She surreptitiously shot little peeks at Darin, with his movie-star chiseled jaw and deep-set blue eyes. His dark blond hair hung a little long over his collar, with a lock that fell across his forehead in an endearing manner that made her want to reach up and brush it back. He periodically flashed her a secret smile when no one appeared to be watching, and his dazzling smile could light up a room, as well as set her heart to skittering. He wore an open-collared brilliant blue shirt that brought out the blue in his eyes, and a pair of expensive-looking tan slacks.

She had worn an outfit much too elegant for a faculty meeting, although thankfully, nobody had mentioned it. A few startled looks had been exchanged when she entered the room wearing a stylish black cocktail dress rather than her usual tailored suit, but she'd avoided the questioning eyes. Fortunately, she'd arrived just as the meeting started, sparing her from having to explain.

"Any questions?"

Startled out of her daydreaming, Kendra looked up. Finally! The old goat looked around the table.

If anyone asks a question, I may have to strangle them. Kendra cast a quick look around the group, hoping her eyes sent the message to keep quiet.

"Yes, Dr. Cochran, I have a question," piped up another professor who liked to show off his intellectual acuity in front of an audience.

Kendra almost groaned out loud, as she pointedly looked at her watch. She slumped in her chair while the second professor asked what surely had to be a profound question in his mind, and Dr. Cochran expounded thoroughly on the subject.

Another man cleared his throat when Dr. Cochran finished. "Perhaps we should defer other questions that don't pertain to the group as a whole to be brought up privately after the meeting?"

"Yes, yes, of course," Dr. Cochran agreed.

Chairs slid back with the sound of collective chair legs swishing across the carpet, and people hopped up, scurrying out of the room, leaving only a handful of faculty members behind to continue conversing.

Darin lingered just outside the door waiting for her. She grinned when she saw him, and she motioned for him to hurry and escape. Once outside, Kendra let out the pent-up laughter that had threatened to explode all through the tedious past two hours.

"Some things are the same everywhere," said Darin, taking hold of her elbow to steer her toward his car. "I was hoping meetings at a smaller college wouldn't be as dreary, but I was wrong."

He guided her to a late-model Mercedes and opened the passenger door. Kendra slid in, taking in the luxurious new-car scent as she sank into the buttery leather seat. Darin slid easily into the driver's seat, closed the door, and then sneezed.

"Bless you," Kendra said.

A fit of sneezing overtook him as he released one sneeze after another. Tears pooled in his eyes as he continued. Finally spent, he reached for a tissue from the console between them, wiped his eyes, and blew his nose.

"Gracious! Are you allergic to something?" Kendra's brows knitted in concern.

"Cats," he wheezed. "You don't have a cat, do you?"

Kendra's heart seized and she closed her eyes, drawing in a deep breath. "Yes, I do. I'm so sorry. I must have some cat hair on my dress." Although she had gone over her clothing carefully, Seymour's fur and her black dress matched. "I could go home and change."

He shook his head. "No, I'll just roll down the window. It didn't bother me in the meeting room. It's probably because we're in a small, confined space." Darin started the engine and pressed the electronic window button, allowing the fresh air to circulate through the vehicle.

Great. I either cause men bodily harm or make them ill. She sat cocooned in guilt as they exited the parking lot onto the main road. The rushing air through the moving car made conversation difficult, so she remained mostly silent as her carefully coiffed hair blew and tangled around her face. She had no doubt she would look like she'd been caught in a hurricane when they reached the restaurant. Plus, Darin already had one strike against him. She couldn't date a man who was allergic to cats. Could she? Maybe if he took a Zyrtec or something before they went out, they could work around this problem.

"Would you like to stop at a pharmacy and pick up an antihistamine?" she yelled over the wind.

He glanced over at her. "That might be a good idea."

"There's a drug store on the next block." She pointed straight ahead.

Darin nodded and steered the car through the intersection and into the parking lot. "I'll be right back," he said, as he jumped from the car and sneezed again.

Kendra sighed as she waited in the car. This date wasn't starting out so well. She looked into the mirror and grimaced at her hair, which had looked so perfect when she'd styled it earlier. Taking a brush from her purse, she tried to tame the recalcitrant curls into a semblance of order while waiting.

Darin emerged from the store bearing a white bag, from which he extracted a bottle. He twisted off the top and downed two pills dry before climbing back into the car.

"Are you supposed to take two?" Kendra asked.

"With my allergies, I need all the help I can get." He started the engine again but didn't roll up the windows.

Kendra placed a hand around her blowing hair and endured the rest of the uncomfortable ride in silence.

Once they reached the restaurant, Darin parked and came around to open her door. She reached out her hand for him to help her, but he didn't take it.

"No offense, but I don't want to touch you and inadvertently transfer cat dander from you to me," he said.

Kendra blinked and sat for a moment before exiting the car. *So now I'm untouchable?* She supposed a goodnight kiss was out of the question. And Darin had such luscious-looking lips. It appeared even a goodnight handshake was out of the question. How she'd fantasized about those gorgeous lips. Her shoulders slightly drooping, she walked next to him into the restaurant, careful not to accidentally brush against him.

She perked up a little at the opulent atmosphere of the establishment. Elegant tables covered in white damask cloths and set with expensive dinnerware and crystal were perfectly positioned to allow for privacy and intimacy. A wine bottle sporting a lit candle served as a centerpiece. Muted lighting and soft, classical music set a tone of relaxed sophistication. Beautiful paintings of Italy covered the walls, and Kendra had no doubt they were expensive. Tendrils of realistic-appearing greenery trailed from dark wood dividers, and racked wine bottles lined the back wall next to the kitchen. Waiters clad in black tuxedos carried out their duties in hushed, unhurried mode. Kendra's stomach rumbled at the delicious-smelling spicy aromas that wafted through the air. She had never eaten in such a fancy restaurant.

Darin gave his name to the maître d', who bowed and led them to a table overlooking a magnificent manmade lake with a waterfall fountain in the center. The maître d' pulled out Kendra's chair and placed her cloth napkin in her lap.

He handed them a wine list, but Darin waved him aside and said, "Just bring us a bottle of your best Chianti."

"Very good, sir." The maître d' bowed again and turned to go.

"Uh, excuse me, sir, one minute." The man stopped and waited. Kendra started to reach across the table to get Darin's attention, then drew her hand back quickly. "Uh, Darin, I don't drink, and I'm not sure you should mix alcohol with antihistamines."

Darin shot her an annoyed look. "Kendra, you can't have fine Italian cuisine without wine."

Kendra lowered her eyes, feeling crude and unsophisticated.

"And don't worry about the antihistamines. They're safe. They're just over-the-counter." He nodded toward the maître d' to confirm his order.

She tried to hide her concern. *You're the biochemist.* But Kendra knew that just because a medication was over-the-counter didn't make it safe to mix with alcohol.

A waiter appeared at their table to fill their water goblets and point out the specials. After he handed them menus and left, Darin settled back in his chair and looked around.

"This place is certainly not on a par with some of the restaurants in Boston, but for a small town, it'll do."

"So, you're from Boston?" Kendra leaned forward, careful not to get too far into Darin's space, lest she bring on a sneezing attack. Interesting. He didn't have a New England accent.

"Well, I didn't grow up there. I grew up in Los Angeles. But I did my post-graduate work at Northwestern and stayed on to teach." He sat back and took a sip of water. "Have you ever been to Boston?"

"No, I haven't, but I would like to." Kendra smiled at him.

"You would love it. So much to see and do. The arts, the symphony, the museums"—he waved his hand for emphasis—"you name it, culturally, Boston has it." A sardonic grin twitched his lips. "Certainly not like here."

Defensiveness rose in her chest.

"This little backwater town bores me to death."

The defensiveness threatened to turn into full-fledged anger. "Then why are you here?" She narrowed her eyes.

He rolled his eyes. "My grandfather had a place here. He died a few weeks ago, and I had to come out and settle his affairs. It seemed a good time to take a sabbatical, while at the same time allowing me to see how some of the smaller colleges operate." He gave a brittle laugh which indicated Blalock was certainly substandard.

Before she could respond, the waiter approached to take their order.

"I'm sorry, I haven't had a chance to look at the menu yet," she said, her appetite diminishing by the minute.

Darin reached over and took her menu. "Allow me." He then proceeded to rattle off an order in rapid Italian.

Her jaw dropped. She didn't know whether to be more stunned that he spoke fluent—at least she supposed it was fluent—Italian, or that he had the audacity to order for her.

The waiter replied in Italian and left the table.

"You speak Italian?" She didn't know why she asked. He obviously did.

He shot her a supercilious look. "Yes. My parents moved to Italy a few years ago. I spent all my summers with them." His gaze settled on a place beyond her shoulder. "Italy. Now there's a place that has everything you could ever want. The Italians really know how to live. And the wine! It's beyond anything you could ever imagine."

She didn't know what to say, so she remained quiet while he continued to regale her with the superior virtues of Italy compared to the United States. Although she wouldn't mind seeing Italy, his attitude in the way he described the country lessened her desire. Darin's good looks seemed to be diminishing by the minute along with her appetite.

The maître d' appeared with their wine, making a huge display of uncorking the bottle and pouring a small quantity into a glass for Darin's inspection. Darin, in turn, made a huge display of swirling, sniffing, and tasting the product before pronouncing it acceptable. The maître d' then poured wine into both of their glasses before taking his leave.

Kendra took a sip. Not being a wine connoisseur, she didn't have much experience with which to judge the beverage. Besides, she didn't particularly care for wine, as she had tried to tell Darin earlier before being dismissed.

Darin sipped slowly as if evaluating each drop. "Well, it can't compare to Italian wine, but then what can?"

Kendra decided to change the subject. "So, you're only here temporarily."

He laughed. "Yes, thank goodness. I can't wait to get back to Boston."

Her gut clenched. *How about tonight*? His disdain for her city was becoming boorish. She raised her chin. "I rather like living in a small town."

His eyebrows shot up. "Seriously? How long have you been here?"

"Twenty years. My parents moved here when I was twelve to have a simpler, slower lifestyle. My first few years were spent in New York City, believe it or not."

He stared at her as if she had told him she was from Mars. "You mean your parents deliberately left the Big Apple to move *here*?"

She fixed her eyes on his. "Yes. And I'm glad they

did."

He shook his head. "To each his own, I guess."

"Yeah, I guess." Kendra looked away and studied other patrons.

The sound of Darin's phone broke the tense air between them. Without saying, "Excuse me," he answered and launched into a long, one-sided conversation.

Kendra's irritation at his rudeness spiked with every moment he chattered away, ignoring her. Not that she particularly wanted his attention, especially his disparagement of her chosen place to live, but still . . .

When the waiter placed their food before them, Darin finally wrapped up the conversation. "Look," he said into the phone, "I've got to go. I'll give you a call tomorrow." He smiled and replaced his phone in his shirt pocket, seeming to suddenly realize Kendra still sat across the table from him.

"That was my stockbroker. He's also a good friend of mine," Darin said, by way of explanation.

"Must have been some hot stock tips," Kendra muttered. She picked up her fork and stabbed at whatever it was that Darin had ordered for her. She really wasn't sure.

"He's the best," Darin said, pouring himself another liberal glass of wine. "I could hook you up with him if you'd like."

"That's okay." She brought her fork to her mouth and busied herself with chewing.

"I hope you have a good financial advisor." Darin took a bite of his meal. "Well, it's not true Italy, but for this area, it's not bad."

Kendra refused to ask what they were eating. As it

was, she couldn't taste anything anyway, and her stomach rebelled at her sending anything its way. "I do. My father."

Darin almost choked on his wine. "Your father?"

"Yes. He's very good at managing money." She forced another bite down her tight throat and chased it with a large gulp of water.

"But is he a professional financial advisor?" Darin polished off his wine and reached for the bottle. He held it her way, questioning whether she wanted more. At her head shake and gesture toward her barely touched glass, he shrugged and poured more for himself. "I mean," he continued, "it's paramount to have someone who knows what they're doing managing your portfolio."

Her portfolio? "He and Mom do okay."

Darin took a huge bite. With his mouth full, he said, "You know, I wish you'd consider moving to Boston. I could introduce you to so much more than you'll ever get here."

She gave him a thin smile. "Thanks, but I've lived in the big city. I'm happy where I am. I like the intimacy of a small college where I can get to know my students, rather than lecture to a crowd of hundreds."

"Well, if you ever change your mind, I'll put in a good word for you at Northeastern."

The meal seemed to drag on, as the contents of the wine bottle disappeared, and Darin's words became more slurred.

"Darin," she said, as they stood to leave. "I don't think the wine and the antihistamines mixed well. Why don't you let me drive?"

He weaved a little bit and replied, "I'm fine.

Besides, nobody drives my car but me."

A sick feeling settled in her stomach. She did not want to get in a car with an impaired man. She also did not want to see him get behind the wheel of a car, but she wasn't going to fight him for his keys. Walking next to him, yet careful not to reach out her hand to steady him, as she wanted to do, her mind churned with how to deal with this predicament.

Ricky stopped his truck at the red light at the intersection of Rutherford and Holmes Boulevard on his way home. Drumming his fingers on the steering wheel, he glanced over to his right. A flash of red hair in the parking lot of the fancy restaurant on the corner caught his eye. No, it couldn't be. Not *her*. Why was that woman suddenly everywhere?

As he continued to watch, his eye was drawn to her date. It figured. A slick, pretty boy. A jolt of jealousy walloped him from out of nowhere, surprising and irritating him. As he wrestled with the strange sensation, he realized something wasn't right. Pretty Boy was drunk. And Kendra appeared to be in distress.

He sighed and turned his truck into the lot, pulling alongside the couple.

Rolling down his window, he called, "Do you need some help?"

Kendra's eyes went wide. "Ricky? What are you doing here?"

He inclined his head in Pretty Boy's direction. "Do you need a lift home?"

Relief flooded her face, but the smile slipped away, replaced by a frown. "Yes, but I don't think Darin should drive."

Ricky put the truck in park and hopped out, placing his Stetson on his head. "Hey, pal," he said to Pretty Boy. "Why don't you let me drive you home?"

Darin stopped and squinted at him. "Who are *you*?"

"Ricky's a friend of mine," Kendra said quickly.

"Yeah? Well, I can drive jus' fine, cowboy." Darin wobbled toward his car.

Ricky put a restraining hand on his arm. "I don't think so. Come on let me—"

Darin turned and swung a fist at Ricky's jaw. Ricky deftly ducked out of the way, then pinned Darin's arms behind his back. "Come on, you're going with me."

Kendra stood rooted to the spot.

"You, too." Ricky looked at her and jerked his head toward his truck.

Grateful, Kendra followed, staying clear of Darin's protesting body.

Ricky opened the back door to his truck and thrust Darin in, none too gently.

"Hey, you stupid hick cowboy! You can't do this. It's kidnapping."

Hoping Darin didn't decide to throw up in the back of his truck, Ricky slammed the door behind him and opened the door for Kendra. Taking her hand, he helped her into the high cab.

"This truck stinks. It smells like a filthy barnyard." Darin spoke the last of his slurred words into his shoulder as his head sagged.

"It smells like a drunk playboy," Ricky mumbled under his breath.

Kendra's hand flew to her mouth, smothering a

giggle.

Darin passed out before they exited the parking lot.

"So, where does Pretty Boy live?" Ricky asked.

"I don't know." Kendra shrugged.

He shot her a skeptical look. "You don't know?"

"No, this is our first . . . and last date."

Ricky ran a hand over his face. "Swell. So, what should we do with him?"

Kendra glanced over the seat at her date. Mr. Dreamy? Hah. More like Mr. Nightmare. "I don't especially want to go through his wallet to see if his address is in there. Besides, it's probably not updated. He's just here for a short time." She chewed on her lip for a moment. "Look, why don't you drop me back by the restaurant, and I'll drive his car to the college. He can spend the night in his car."

Ricky shrugged. "Sounds good to me. Although I'd prefer to leave him in a ditch by the side of the road."

"That makes two of us." She cast a doleful look at Ricky. "Thanks for stopping. I didn't know what I was going to do."

Ricky nodded. "I hope you weren't planning to get in the car with Pretty Boy."

She smiled at his reference to Darin. "No, I would have called a cab. But I didn't know how I was going to prevent him from getting in the car and driving away."

They re-entered the lot and Kendra directed Ricky to Darin's car.

"Mercedes. Figures." Ricky got out of the truck and Kendra followed without waiting for him to open her door. *Yeah, I forgot. Liberated woman.* "I don't suppose you know where his keys are."

"I believe he put them in his front pocket."

Ricky opened the back door and patted Pretty Boy's pockets for the keys. Darin didn't even rouse. Ricky tossed the keys to Kendra. "I'll follow you."

She nodded and unlocked Darin's door, slipping into the driver's seat. Ricky waited for her to pull out, then followed her to the campus. Kendra parked under a street light.

"Hope security finds him and calls the cops," she said, as she opened the back door to the Mercedes.

Ricky worked to extract Pretty Boy from the back seat of his truck. It wasn't easy, considering Darin was deadweight. Ricky propped the unconscious man against the side of the truck and leaned into him so he didn't collapse on the ground. "Help me get him in the car," he grunted.

With Ricky on one side, Kendra positioned herself on Darin's other side and steadied him. "I hope I get cat hair all over him."

"What?" Ricky panted, as they dragged Darin to the car.

"He's allergic to cats. Apparently, you can't completely keep your clothes free of cat dander. He had a sneezing attack because of my cat when we were in the closed car. We had to stop and pick up antihistamines." She helped shove Darin into the back seat of the Mercedes and Ricky slammed the door.

Ricky bent over, his hands on his knees catching his breath. "And he mixed drugs with alcohol," he puffed. "What a jerk." Ricky shot a glance at Kendra. Why wasn't she out of breath? Probably because he'd done all the heavy work.

She nodded. "I tried to tell him." She glanced at

Darin's slumped body in the Mercedes. "At least the weather's mild. He'll be okay, although I wouldn't be particularly broken up if he froze to death. Too bad it's not January." Turning back to Ricky, she said, "I feel so foolish. But never having been out with the guy, I didn't expect this to happen. Once again, you've come to my rescue." Her eyes searched his. "Thank you."

A cool night breeze stirred the air. Ricky didn't know if it was the breeze or the strange look in Kendra's eyes that caused a shiver to travel up his spine. He took off his hat and made a mocking bow. "My pleasure. At least you didn't injure me this time."

Kendra laughed. "You're right. But we haven't made it out of the parking lot yet."

"I'll let you get a safe distance away before I leave. And I'll stand over by the building so you don't run me down."

She laughed again. "It's a deal. Seriously, thank you." She stepped closer and gave him a stiff, one-armed hug. That tantalizing floral scent she'd worn the day she fell on him heightened his senses.

Ricky tensed. Her touch sent unwanted tingles through his body. "Yeah, you're welcome. Now get away from me before you hurt me," he said gruffly.

She grinned. He watched her walk to her car and get in. Feigning fear, he backed up out of her way. She waved as she pulled out, and he gave her a salute in return.

Climbing back into his truck, he shook his head. He didn't want these feelings.

CHAPTER SIX

Kendra replayed the evening in her mind as she drove home. How could Mr. Dreamy have turned out to be such a creep? To think she'd salivated over that guy! She only hoped she wouldn't keep running into him at school. She would keep her distance the best she could, but it was inevitable their paths would cross sooner or later. What would his reaction be when he faced her again? It didn't matter. She was done with him. Why was she such a poor judge of men? It seemed all the academic types she'd dated, starting with Aaron, had turned out to be full of themselves. Maybe that was the problem. Maybe she should look elsewhere. But where? Most of the men she knew were from work or church.

Ricky's face sprang to the forefront of her brain, and she felt a smile tugging on the corners of her mouth. Although rough around the edges, and despite their first encounter, he appeared to be a gentleman. He had an undefinable character about him that made her feel she was safe with him and she could trust him. He'd certainly shown up at the right time tonight, and she'd appreciated his help. No, not help. He'd rescued her. *Oh, Kendra, don't be so dramatic. You weren't completely helpless.* Sure, she could have called a cab and tried to talk Darin into letting the cab take them home. But what if he'd become belligerent? She'd seen how he'd acted when Ricky offered to take him home. He'd actually tried to punch Ricky. Kendra said a quick prayer of thanks that Darin's swing had not connected with Ricky's face. Otherwise, this would be one more instance of Ricky getting injured whenever she was around.

She admired Ricky's strength and sense in handling the difficult situation. Not only had he easily evaded Darin's misplaced blow, he'd taken charge and kept the intoxicated man from causing further damage to either himself or others. The image of a hero riding in on his white horse to save the day flashed through her mind, and she snickered at the picture of herself as the damsel in distress.

She wondered about Ricky's background. Where had he come from? She'd lived here for twenty years, but up until a short while ago, she'd never seen him. She supposed she could ask Darcy. But then Darcy might get the wrong idea. After all, Kendra only had a mild curiosity about him. It wasn't as if she was interested in him as a *man*. Although, good looks aside—and if she were completely honest with herself, his thick, black hair, dark eyes, and strong jaw made for one handsome guy—she'd never met a man quite like him. Would it be so wrong to want to know him better? His lop-sided grin and adorable dimple only added to his charm and must certainly attract the attention of many women. Was he involved with someone? Chances were he was.

Besides, a romantic interest would never work between them. They were too different. She had a suspicion he viewed her as a useless intellectual and held a certain amount of contempt toward her. And, for her part, how would she feel about being with someone beneath her educational level? Her snobbish pride reared its ugly head again. She huffed out a little laugh. Her experience with men on her academic level hadn't worked out so well. And, for that matter, why was it perfectly okay for men with higher education to be with women who weren't on their intellectual level, but the converse was not true? Who made those rules, anyway? Could a relationship like that work? She tried to think of a couple she knew who fit that description, but couldn't come up with anyone.

Would Ricky fit in with her academic circle of acquaintances? Hardly. Would she fit in with his cowboy lifestyle? Hardly. She had only ridden a horse for the first time a few months ago and still wasn't overly comfortable around the big beasts. Still, she couldn't deny her attraction to the man. Maybe she could discreetly inquire of Darcy whether or not Ricky was seeing someone.

Oh, Kendra, you silly woman. You're just reacting to his gallantry tonight. That's all.

Ricky got undressed and crawled into bed, bone tired, yet exhilarated. For some reason, coming to Kendra's aid tonight had made him feel heroic. He chuckled to himself at his inflated ego. As if someone like her couldn't take care of herself and needed his manly intervention. Still, even though Pretty Boy had turned out to be a loser, Ricky saw what type of man attracted Kendra. Sharp, flashy, suave, sophisticated—all the things he wasn't. She obviously liked men who took her to expensive restaurants like La Traviata, places Ricky could never afford. Even if he could afford fancy places like La Traviata, he would not feel comfortable eating in such an uppity restaurant. He'd probably use the wrong fork and be reprimanded by a haughty waiter. So, there was no use even speculating about Kendra. But he couldn't deny the chemistry he felt with her. He had to laugh. Chemistry like oil and water described the two of them better. Hydrophobic and hydrophilic. She'd probably be surprised to find he even *knew* those scientific words. He'd never tell her.

For some reason, his mind drifted back to Lily, and, for once, he allowed it to go there. Generally, he shut down every stray thought of her. Lily was in his past. His past was dead and gone. Now, Ricky tried to live in the present, in the moment. The future loomed ahead, unknown and uncertain, but he had no desire to plan, as he had in his previous life. Before, he'd had everything mapped out with a timeline, down to the last detail. Now, nothing mattered but getting through each day.

Didn't the Bible say something about not worrying about tomorrow because tomorrow had enough worry of its own? Something like that. Bible verses kept popping into his head, which aggravated him. He supposed that having grown up in a Christian home and being forced to go to church all his life had left a mark. But Ricky couldn't buy into that philosophy about God having a plan for his life anymore. Not with the way God allowed the evil in the world to prevail.

He closed his eyes, and a vision of Lily became so

real in his mind's eye that his breath caught. He could almost reach out and touch her. Although the vision jabbed at his heart like a hot poker, he let it remain. For months after he'd lost her, he'd walked around dead inside. His brain just hadn't sent the message to his heart to stop beating and his lungs to stop breathing. He didn't know how a heart could break so badly and still function. Guilt wrapped around his gut like a strangling vine. A hot tear escaped from his right eye and trailed down his cheek.

"We got the apartment!" Lily squealed, the minute Ricky walked in the door. Her sky-blue eyes twinkled with excitement. She ran across the room and threw her arms around her neck.

"What? You're kidding." He buried his face in her silky, ash-blonde air and inhaled deeply of her clean, cherry almond shampoo. Raising his head so he could look in her eyes, he asked, "When can we move in?"

"Next month." She raised up on tiptoe and planted a firm kiss on his lips. "Can you believe it?"

He tilted her chin toward his mouth and went back for seconds. Finally, coming up for air, she broke the embrace and pulled him toward the kitchen.

"I can't wait to get out of this dump. Four long years."

Ricky looked around at the peeling paint, the scuffed, outdated linoleum floor, and the bare pipes that rattled whenever hot water ran through them. Not to mention the paper-thin walls. "Me, too, babe. Mm, what smells so good?"

She grabbed a pair of potholders from the counter and bent to remove something from the oven. "Your favorite. Prime rib.”

“Prime rib? That must have cost—”

Setting the roasting pan on the stove, she turned and pressed a finger against his lips. “I splurged. We needed to celebrate.” She went back to retrieve baked potatoes. “Besides, once your thesis is approved and you have your doctorate, we’ll be able to afford more than canned tuna.”

He wrapped her in a hug and laid his cheek on top of her head. She fit so perfectly against him. “I love you, Lil.”

“I love you, too,” she murmured against his chest.

If he imagined hard enough, he could almost smell the scent of her cherry almond shampoo. The flow of tears continued in a steady stream. If they could only have stayed in that moment forever—a rare moment in which all was right with the world. The future stretched before them, exciting and promising, and their love would only grow stronger if that were possible. All the sacrifices, all their plans about to come to fruition. If he had only known, he would have cherished the everyday moments more.

CHAPTER SEVEN

"So," Kendra said, pretending to only be making conversation. "Ricky had to come to my rescue again the other night." By a fortuitous coincidence, she and Darcy had nursery duty during the morning service. It seemed a good time to pump her friend for information without everyone else overhearing.

Darcy placed a baby in a swing and turned the switch on low. "Really? What happened?" She returned to the rocking chair next to where Kendra fed another infant a bottle. A children's Bible songs CD played quietly in the background as several toddlers played on the floor around their feet.

Kendra related the details of her disastrous date.

"How awful. I'm glad Ricky just happened to see you," Darcy said.

"Yeah. Things could have turned out a lot worse."

"So, have you bumped into this guy, Darin, since then?"

Kendra pressed her lips together. "Unfortunately, yes. To his credit, he did apologize. Then he had the audacity to ask if I wanted to go out again."

Darcy's eyes widened. "You're kidding. What did

you say?" She gently broke up a squabble between two toddlers fighting over a toy and re-directed their attention to two identical toys, one for each of them.

"I said I was busy that night." Kendra tipped up the empty bottle and set it on the table next to her chair. She placed a burp rag over her shoulder and positioned the infant upright, patting his back.

"And what did he say?"

Kendra grinned. "He said he hadn't mentioned a specific night."

"And?"

"I said 'exactly.'"

Darcy snickered. "Oh, Kendra, I'm so sorry for your bad experience."

Kendra steered the discussion back to Ricky. "Yes, but as you said, I was lucky Ricky happened by." The baby let out a huge belch, and both women giggled. Without looking at Darcy, she said, "He seems like a nice man."

"He is," Darcy agreed. One of the toddlers now had both toys, refusing to share. Darcy sighed and directed them to the children's table, where she distributed crayons and paper.

Drat. Darcy wasn't going to elaborate. "Where's he from?" Kendra asked.

Darcy shot her a sharp look, but Kendra pretended not to notice. "I'm not sure. Somewhere back east, I think."

"How did he end up here?"

Merriment danced in Darcy's eyes, and Kendra knew her subterfuge wasn't working. "I'm not sure about that, either. He's been with Ben for a couple of years, but Ricky keeps pretty much to himself. He doesn't seem to get close to people." She removed a crayon from one of the toddler's mouths and showed him how to color on the paper.

Kendra blew out a breath as she continued to absently pat the infant's back.

"And, as far as I know, he's not seeing anyone." Darcy grinned.

Warmth rose in Kendra's cheeks. "I didn't ask whether he was seeing anyone."

"I know. I thought I'd save you the trouble."

Kendra's cheeks flamed now, and not for the first time, she rued her pale complexion. "I'm not looking to date him, Darcy. We're totally incompatible."

"Then why are you blushing?"

"I'm . . . I'm not. It's just warm in here, that's all." Kendra rose and deposited the now-sleeping infant in a crib.

"I'm sorry for poking fun at you," Darcy said to Kendra's back. "Although you deserve it for all the teasing you did to Molly over Ben."

Darcy referred to their other friend, Molly's, initial reaction when she first met Ben—long before Darcy entered the picture. Kendra had never let Molly live down the fact that she had found Ben attractive, although there had never been anything between them.

Kendra faced her. "It was her own fault for going on and on about how handsome he was. You know how Molly is. She can't keep anything to herself. Everybody knows what she's thinking."

Darcy laughed. "True. Poor Tim." Gregarious Molly and shy Tim in their Sunday school class had recently become an item. "Talk about incompatible. They're nothing alike, but their relationship seems to be working just fine for them."

The mention of Molly and Tim pairing up reminded Kendra of her single status, and a longing she couldn't define gnawed at her insides.

"Look, Kendra, Ricky's a nice man. You could do worse. You *have* done worse."

Kendra shoved an errant curl from her face. "Touché. But Ricky and I have nothing in common. I don't think he even likes me."

"Do you want me to ask Ben to ask Ricky how he feels about you?" Darcy removed the crayons from the child determined to chew on them and replaced them with a picture book.

"Of course not!" Kendra flattened her lips and scowled at her friend. The very idea was humiliating. "This is all so high-schoolish. I'm thirty-two years old, Darcy, not fourteen."

"Well, sometimes it doesn't hurt to give things a little push." Darcy rose, snagged a dropped pacifier off the floor, rinsed it off, and plopped it back into the mouth of an infant on the floor who had spit it out and was starting to fuss.

"Thanks, but don't push me. Or him." Kendra busied herself with folding baby blankets.

"Okay. But just in case you want to know, Ben and I have to go to Jackson Hole on Saturday afternoon. We should be gone a couple of hours."

Kendra turned. "So?"

"You still haven't returned the punch bowl." Darcy gave her a knowing look.

Kendra's hands flew to her cheeks. "Oh, I'm sorry. I completely forgot. I should have brought it to church today."

Darcy pursed her lips. "That's not what I was getting at."

Kendra's brows drew together.

"Ricky will be at the ranch," Darcy said pointedly. "I could tell him you'll be dropping by."

Kendra hoped the fire burning in her eyes scorched her friend.

Kendra stared at the punch bowl sitting on her kitchen table. She would not, *not* stoop so low as to make up a flimsy excuse to see Ricky. How desperate did Darcy think she was, anyway, to resort to something so obvious? Hadn't Kendra told Darcy not to treat her like a teenager with a crush? Yet the punch bowl sat there mocking her, and she did need to return it. She'd completely forgotten about it, and the embarrassment of not having returned it in a timely manner made her annoyed with herself. Generally a responsible woman, Kendra didn't know how she had let it slip her mind. But the obvious suggestion to return it *today* so she'd be sure to run into Ricky rankled her.

Why did paired-up couples have to meddle in the love lives of their single friends? Why couldn't they leave well enough alone? Couldn't they see how awkward their interference was? *Love life*? Kendra snorted. She had no love life. Maybe Darcy *was* just trying to move things along a little, thinking she was doing a favor for her poor, old maid friend. Kendra bristled at the idea. This wasn't the last century, for heaven's sake. Today, it was perfectly acceptable for women to remain happily single without a man to complete them. She had been content with her life before everyone in her circle of friends had become couples, making her feel like an oddball.

She just needed to re-adjust her thinking, that's all. Or get new single friends. Kendra plopped down in a kitchen chair. She had a lot of things to do today besides driving all the way out to Whispering Winds Ranch. She had to . . .

Blast it all! Kendra snatched the punch bowl and her purse, slamming the door behind her.

I'm just going to leave the punch bowl on the back porch. I am not going to go looking for Ricky. But even as the words formed in her head, her heart betrayed her by speeding up at the thought of seeing him again. She banged her hands on her steering wheel. Treacherous organ! This behavior was so unlike her. She'd never acted this way, even in junior high. Mentally scolding herself for her foolishness, she tried to enumerate the reasons, yet again, why a relationship with Ricky was out of the question. She had already exhausted most of the arguments. Aside from a strong physical attraction—one that seemed to be getting stronger all the time—they had nothing in common, as she had pointed out repeatedly, both to Darcy and to herself. A relationship with a man like that would only bring heartache in the end, so it was best not to hope for something that shouldn't start in the first place. She needed to put him out of her mind.

She didn't need to have a male partner simply because everyone else in her immediate circle of single friends had gone over to the other side. Kendra could redefine herself as the cool aunt to all their kids, when they had kids, that is. Besides, at the age of thirty-two, she was set in her ways. Kendra liked things the way she wanted them. She didn't want to have to answer to anyone else or make accommodations for someone else's idiosyncrasies. And for companionship, she had Seymour, who was both male and low maintenance.

"I like my life just the way it is," she muttered under her breath as she approached the driveway to the ranch. "So don't you go messing it up."

How ridiculous. Ricky had hardly been camped on her doorstep waiting to sweep her off her feet. So why should she assume he wanted to mess up her life? Making assumptions about Ricky's intentions toward her would be even more humiliating if he ever guessed her wayward thoughts. He would probably laugh at her impudence for entertaining such notions.

Well, it was about time she showed up! Darcy had told Ricky that Kendra would be coming by to return the punch bowl while she and Ben were gone. Ricky had been puttering close to the house all day so he wouldn't miss her arrival. No, not puttering. He'd had legitimate work to do, although he'd taken his sweet time in doing so, and he was running out of excuses to avoid riding out to the pasture to do his twice-daily evaluation of the cattle. Besides, it wasn't like he had to be here to receive the borrowed item. The bowl would be perfectly safe on the porch. To the best of his knowledge, there hadn't been any recent outbreaks of punch bowl thefts.

He despised his adolescent reaction to the woman. Not since he'd fallen for Lily in high school had he ever felt this way about a female, and he was too old to start now. But as the crunch of gravel under Kendra's tires reached his ears, he found himself grinning. Then he told himself to stop it. Deliberately wiping the stupid grin off his face, he replaced it with what he hoped was a stern expression.

He could have just walked out and accepted the returned item from her without her having to get out of the car. But then she could make a quick getaway, and he didn't want that. He waited until he heard the slam of her car door and the muted steps from her sneakers until he appeared by the side of the house.

"Hi," he said, trying his best to act surprised to see her there.

She jumped at his greeting, and for a split second, he hoped she didn't drop the bowl and shatter it.

"Oh! You startled me. I didn't see you there." She stood on the back patio wearing a pair of modest shorts and a green T-shirt that made her green eyes seem even more striking.

"Sorry." He pulled his Stetson off his head and pushed a lock of dark hair from his brow. "I heard the car drive up and came to check."

Her giveaway blush was becoming all too familiar, and he chuckled inwardly. "I came to return this," she said as if the wieldy bowl in her hands weren't obvious.

"How did the reception go?" He assumed a casual posture of leaning against the side of the house, crossing one ankle over the other, hands buried deep in his pockets.

"The reception?" She blinked, seeming to have forgotten the occasion for the use of the bowl. "Oh, yes. It went fine, thank you."

"Good."

They both stood awkwardly seeming to wait for the other to make a move.

"And how's Pretty Boy?"

Kendra rolled her eyes. "He doesn't seem any worse for the wear. Although he had the nerve to ask me out again."

Ricky nodded. "Gotta give the guy points for chutzpah."

She shifted the bowl to her other hip. "I suppose Darin's good looks cover a multitude of sins."

Ricky didn't know why her reference to Pretty Boy's good looks irked him. He moved to take the heavy bowl from her. "So, you think he's good-looking?"

Kendra's sharp eyes zeroed in on him. "I guess, in a—what did you call him? A playboy sort of way. Why?"

It was Ricky's turn to feel the heat in his face. Fortunately, with his sun-weathered skin, it didn't show as obviously as her blushes did. "I take it you turned down his generous offer." Ricky elected to ignore her question as to why he cared whether or not she found Darin good-looking.

She snorted. "Do I *look* stupid? Don't answer that."

Ricky grinned. "I do give you more credit than that. I guess we've all been burned at least once on a bad date."

Kendra gave him a sardonic smile. "I'd love to hear about *yours*."

"I'll just bet you would," he said, as he brushed past her to open the kitchen door. He set the bowl on the table and turned, finding she had followed him inside.

"Well?" she prodded. "I'm waiting to hear about your bad date."

"Some secrets I'll take to my grave, thank you."

"That's not fair. You've seen me at *my* worst." She planted her hands on her hips.

"How about something to drink?" he said, changing the subject.

She narrowed her eyes at him, but replied, "Sure. Let's raid Ben and Darcy's refrigerator."

Ricky opened the stainless-steel frig and removed two bottles of water as he tried to think of a way to prolong her visit.

Kendra accepted the water and took a long drink. "Thanks. I didn't realize how warm it was today." She held back a crop of curls and ran the sweating bottle over her forehead.

"Yeah, it is warm." *Great. We're talking about the weather.* Well, it had been a while since he'd had to make conversation with a pretty woman. He was a little rusty. *Pretty woman*? Where had *that* come from? He cast a sideways glance at her. Yeah, he supposed she was nice-looking enough in a girl-next-door kind of way. Her coppery-colored curls framed her porcelain-complexioned face most becomingly. Despite her red hair, she bore no freckles—at least none that he could tell without further inspection, which he could not do without being obvious. Unusual. Her telltale pale cheeks flushed a magnificent shade of pink when she was embarrassed. The pink should have clashed with her red hair, but the two colors managed to complement each other nicely. And those green eyes. He had never seen such a brilliant color.

His brain worked feverishly to come up with something scintillating to say. "So," he said, pulling out a chair and plopping down. "How long have you lived in Wyoming?" He took a sip of his water.

She looked a little confused, and he guessed his not-so-covert way of delaying her departure was largely to blame.

"Twenty years. And you?"

"A couple." He gestured toward the chair across from him, and she hesitated.

"Don't you have work you have to get back to?"

He shrugged. "It'll still be there in a few minutes, and I need to take a break. That is unless you have to get home."

She stood for a moment, then pulled out a chair and sat. "No, not really."

"So, where are you from originally?" He played with his bottle cap.

"New York City. My parents moved here because they wanted a simpler, more peaceful place to live and raise their kids."

New York City? Interesting. "Are they still living here?"

Kendra shook her head. "They moved to Florida a few years ago. The winters were becoming too much for them."

"But not for you?"

She smiled. "I love it here. I've visited my parents in Florida, of course, but this is the only place I want to live."

"Yeah, me too."

"What brought you here?"

He should have known her question would be a logical progression in this conversation. But he couldn't go there now. He blew out a breath.

"I needed a change of pace. My grandfather had a

cattle ranch in Montana, and I spent a lot of summers with him when I was a boy. Those were the happiest times in my life." *Well, at least until Lily.* But all those happy times had become so mingled with the tragic end that he couldn't think of one without the other. "I was fortunate to stumble across Whispering Winds Ranch at just the right time."

"I would say Ben was the fortunate one." Sincerity shown in her eyes.

He grinned. "And just what would you know about how good I am at cattle wrangling?"

She laughed. "You've got me there. But I suspect you must be pretty good or Ben wouldn't keep you around."

Ricky was about to say something else when the sound of a vehicle coming up the driveway caught his attention. Rising from the chair, he looked out the window. "They're back." Disappointment colored his tone. He wished he could have had a few more minutes with Kendra.

Kendra stood and moved toward the door. Truck doors slammed, and Mack, Ben's Australian Shepherd, jumped out of the cab and began barking. Kendra quickly went outside to greet them.

"Hey, guys. I brought back your punch bowl."

Even from where he stood on the porch, Ricky could see Kendra's face turning red as if she had been caught in the act of doing something she shouldn't have been doing.

Mack circled her, continuing to bark, as Darcy's lips turned up in a sly grin.

"Mack!" Ben scolded. "Thanks, Kendra, but you really didn't have to . . ." His eyes traveled to where

Ricky stood on the back porch, and Ben exchanged an amused glance with Darcy.

"I've got to go check the cattle," Ricky muttered, striding away toward the barn.

CHAPTER EIGHT

Ben caught up with Ricky out in the pasture. Pulling his horse alongside Ricky's, he said, "Hey, man, sorry if we interrupted something back there."

Ricky shot him what he hoped was a confused look. "What do you mean?" He didn't want Ben prying into his personal life. *Personal life*? He had no personal life. Kendra didn't mean anything to him. And he doubted he meant anything to her. He couldn't even define the strange feelings he had for the woman, let alone have a heart-to-heart discussion about them with someone else—even someone he considered a good friend like Ben. Ricky had never been a "touchy-feely" type of guy, and he sure didn't want to start now.

The corners of Ben's mouth twitched. "Okay, if that's the way you want to play it."

A slow breath escaped Ricky's lips. Yes, that's the way he did want to play it, whatever "it" was. He busied himself with studying the black cattle that grazed contentedly in the warm sunshine, their long tails swishing at flies.

"Look, man, I'm sorry. Whatever is going on between Kendra and you is none of my business."

Ricky turned toward his friend, irritation rising in his chest. "Nothing is going on."

"Well—" Ben took off his hat and swatted at a yellow fly—"she made a special point of coming out here today when she knew Darcy and I were going to be gone."

Hmm. That was interesting. Curiosity got the better of him. "She knew you weren't home?"

Ben nodded. "Darcy specifically mentioned it to her in church the other day."

Very interesting. Ricky felt a grin tug on the right side of his lips, and he squelched it. "We were just talking. I was being friendly. She's *your* friend, after all, not mine." His gaze traveled back to the cattle. "Looks like we're going to need to treat for flies."

"Yeah, we'll do it tomorrow." Ben raised his eyebrows. "She's a nice lady."

Great, they were back on the subject of Kendra. "Yeah, she seems okay, at least when she's not causing physical harm to me. But, as I told you before, I'm not looking." Ricky was happy with his life just the way it was. Simple, uncomplicated. Even though Kendra stirred up long-dead feelings in him, and he enjoyed being in her company, taking a bigger step toward getting involved with her was a whole 'nother issue he preferred to avoid. He'd had his chance at love and he'd blown it, in the worst possible way. He would never find anything remotely close to what he'd lost, and he didn't want to try. He preferred nothing to second-best.

"We're hosting a hayride for some of our church friends next Saturday," Ben said, interrupting Ricky's contemplation.

Good. Finally, a change of subject. "Okay, boss,

what do you need me to do to get ready?"

Ben chuckled. "I'm not asking you to work. I'm inviting you to come."

A strange cadence started up in Ricky's heart. "Uh, thanks, but I don't know. I'd be out of place. I don't know any of those people."

"You know me and Darcy and Kendra. There are only a few others. You'd like them."

Ricky hesitated. "If this is a subtle way of getting me and Kendra together, it isn't very subtle. Besides, I don't get along with church people all that well." He nudged his horse gently to move on ahead.

Ben called after him. "Why not? You get along with Darcy and me."

Ricky noted that Ben deliberately avoided mentioning Kendra.

"What's wrong with church people?"

Ricky stopped and sighed. Ben wasn't going to let this conversation go. "Okay, it's not church people, per se. It's God I have issues with."

Ben caught up to Ricky again. "God? What issues do you have with God?" He shaded his eyes with his hand against the glare of the shifting late-afternoon sun.

Ricky closed his eyes and clenched his jaw. He didn't want to have this discussion. But again, he knew Ben wouldn't let his comment go. Sometimes Ben's persistence could wear a person down. "I don't understand how a loving God can allow all the evil things to happen in this world."

He heard Ben let out a long breath. "Yeah, I know. That's a difficult concept to wrap our minds around." Ben lowered his head for a moment, apparently in thought.

When he looked up again, Ricky lowered his own eyes, not wanting to hear whatever Ben was about to say to try to make sense of something that made no sense. He was glad the sun made it difficult for Ben to see the hardness Ricky felt on his face.

"We have to remember that the evil things in this world are not from God, and sometimes innocent people get caught up in the consequences of that evil."

"But God can stop bad things from happening. Why doesn't He?" Soft lowing came from the cattle, a sound that usually brought peace to Ricky's troubled spirit, but not today. Not with this conversation.

Ben shook his head. "I don't know the answer to that. But He created us with free will, not as robots. And we have to remember that there will always be things in this world we don't understand. That's where faith and trust come in."

Ricky huffed out a humorless laugh. "That's a convenient platitude."

"No, none of it is convenient," Ben said softly. "But I have to trust in Romans 8:28, where it says God can work all things for good to those who love Him and are called according to His purposes. That doesn't mean everything is good, but that God can ultimately use bad circumstances for His glory."

Ricky had heard it all before. He just couldn't apply it to *his* circumstances. There could never be any good that would come out of what happened to Lily. "We'd best get a move on before it gets dark." He spurred his horse into a trot, leaving Ben behind and cutting off further discussion.

Ben watched Ricky ride away. Darkness wouldn't

come for another couple of hours. Ben didn't know much about Ricky's past, but he'd sensed there was something painful in the man's background that he hadn't dealt with. His sudden appearance at Whispering Winds and his reluctance to let anyone get close to him spoke of secrets Ricky held close to his heart. Most of Ben's attempts to get him to open up had been met with firm resistance. Maybe Ben should just let it go. Ricky was an excellent worker—competent, loyal, and dependable. But he seemed broken somehow.

Ben thought he'd seen the tiniest crack in the man's tough shell when he'd literally run into Kendra. She was a good woman, smart and kind. Her attraction to Ricky was obvious. And Ben had seen interest spark in Ricky, as well. Would it be so bad to encourage them to get to know each other better? Still, Ben didn't want to push too hard. If it was God's will, He would work out the way.

CHAPTER NINE

"How about lunch, Kendra?"

Kendra looked up from her lesson notes for her afternoon lecture into the face of Dr. Wade Weber, the lab supervisor.

"I have a class at two," she said, glancing at her watch.

"We can grab a quick bite at the deli around the corner and be back in plenty of time. I've got something I need to discuss with you."

Kendra thought about her yogurt in the refrigerator. A deli sandwich sounded much more appetizing. "Okay, let me shut down my computer and I'll be right with you."

They left the small campus and walked the short distance to the deli. The chilliness of the morning had given way to a warm, pleasant afternoon with the radiant sun beating down from a cloudless, blue sky and warming the concrete under their feet. Kendra struggled to remove her sweater.

"Here, let me help you." Wade reached over to assist her.

"Thanks," she said, taking the sweater from him. "This time of year, I always dress too warmly because

I'm freezing in the morning. Then I burn up later in the day."

"Layering is the way to go."

They reached the deli, and Wade held the door for her. Enticing aromas emanated from the small kitchen, and Kendra found her stomach growling. Busy with her classwork, she hadn't realized how hungry she was.

"There's a spot by the window. Have a seat and I'll put in our orders. What would you like?"

She pondered a moment. "Ham and Swiss on sourdough bread. And a diet cola." Kendra fished in her purse for money.

"It's okay, I've got it."

"Thanks. I'll buy lunch next time." She settled back to wait, her eyes drawn to the street outside. Was that Ricky? For someone she didn't even know existed until a few weeks ago, he sure seemed to be everywhere. She raised her hand to wave, but he ducked around the corner and disappeared.

Ricky caught sight of Kendra walking down the sidewalk with yet another Pretty Boy. This guy looked even more suave and yuppie than the last one. He watched as the man helped her off with her sweater, then opened the door to the café for her. For reasons he couldn't explain, he stood outside to see what they would do next. *Idiot. What do you think they'll do? They're obviously eating lunch.* Still, he couldn't make himself leave.

A frisson of jealousy snaked its way through his body, and he didn't like it. Why should he care who she ate lunch with, even if it was with a sophisticated, good-looking man? That was clearly the type of guy she favored, despite her last experience. Correction. The last experience Ricky was aware of. For all Ricky knew, she could have been on a dozen dates with a dozen different men between Pretty Boy Number One and this guy. He didn't know why the thought bothered him so much, but the idea of her being a player didn't set right. He'd thought there had been a little connection between them the other day. Still, it wasn't enough to get worked up over. He certainly had no claim on Kendra. Nor did he want one.

Ricky's thoughts made him feel like he was back in junior high again, which annoyed him all the more. If the woman was going to get under his skin, he either needed to do something about it or avoid her. Avoiding her hadn't worked, as they kept ending up in the same place at the same time. But what should he do? What did he *want* to do? He wanted these blasted feelings to go away, that's what he wanted.

He'd reasoned with himself repeatedly as to why a relationship with Kendra simply wouldn't work—case in point, the guy she was currently with. She might be nice and kind and all that, but when push came to shove, a woman of her status would not be seriously drawn to a man like him. Even a mutual attraction, if that's what they shared, was not sustainable.

Shoot! She'd spotted him. Like a kid caught with his hand in the cookie jar, he scurried away, pretending not to see her.

"Thanks, Wade," Kendra said, as he set her lunch on the table. "Mm, that looks yummy."

Wade plopped down across from her and took a big bite of his corned beef on rye.

"How're Carmen and the kids?" she asked.

He chewed and smiled at the same time. "All good. Can you believe we're coming up on our tenth anniversary already?"

A bittersweet sensation stabbed at her heart. Why did it seem like everyone around her was happily married? She'd met Wade's wife, Carmen, and their two children on several occasions, and had liked them quite a bit. They were a nice family. Besides, Kendra was the one who'd asked about them. She was happy for all of them. Really. So why did she feel so lonely all of a sudden?

Forcing a smile, she said, "Ten years. Wow. Congratulations." She took a bite of her sandwich and tried to suppress her feelings. "So, what did you want to talk to me about?"

Wade wiped his mouth on his napkin and took a sip of his drink before responding. "I'm having trouble procuring fetal pigs for dissection in the biology lab. I was wondering what you thought about using cats?"

An image of Seymour sprang to her mind. "Cats?"

"Yes, for some reason, obtaining cats is not a problem. I know we've always used fetal pigs in the past. I was just wondering what you thought about making that change."

She took another bite as she mulled over the idea. "I wouldn't personally have any objection, although I do own a cat."

He laughed. "That's just it. I'm wondering with all the political correctness and sensitivity today if using cats might be offensive to some students."

Kendra nodded. "Yes, I see what you mean. Dissecting cats might give them PTSD about Fluffy."

She looked around at the patrons at the next table who sat staring at their table with horrified expressions on their faces. Lowering her voice, she said, "If the reaction from the table next to ours is any indication, I would say we might want to consider another alternative."

He followed her line of sight. "Sorry, I should have kept my voice down. I keep forgetting that talking shop in public is not always agreeable to others."

She grinned. "I do the same thing. I used to gross my father out at the dinner table when I came home and talked about my biology classes. He once turned green and asked me to leave the table when I mentioned we'd studied Lepidoptera that day."

Wade laughed again. "Butterflies?"

"I didn't let him in on that fact at the time. I enjoyed pushing his buttons."

"Humor only a biologist would get." Wade sighed. "Well, I suppose I could always get rats. Although their anatomy is smaller and a little harder to dissect, I don't think too many people are attached to them."

"I agree. And as long as you keep them in the lab, I'll be fine."

"You do know we don't get live specimens. They arrive preserved in formalin."

She smiled. "Yes, I remember those days well. You can never get rid of that smell. That's why I'm glad I'm in the classroom and *you're* in the lab."

"But you miss out on all the fun." He finished his sandwich and wadded up his napkin.

"Sorry, but even pickled rats give me the heebie-jeebies." She took her last sip of soda. "I'd better get back to class. Thanks for the lovely lunchtime

discussion."
"My pleasure. Anytime."

CHAPTER TEN

Ricky drove back to the ranch, out of sorts for reasons he didn't care to analyze. Usually, the majestic scenery of wide-open spaces and snow-capped mountains filled him with peace, and he tried to focus on the beauty of the landscape all around him. He loved the vastness and ruggedness of this area, with so many parks and hiking trails he could easily lose himself in nature. At any given moment he might see elk or bison. It was a far cry from the concrete jungle of New York City. As he drove, he studied the sagebrush by the side of the road, its presence giving authenticity to the fact he really lived in this unique, unspoiled part of the country. Sometimes, even after two years, he had to pinch himself to believe he had managed to land in the most beautiful place he had ever seen.

His sour mood had slowly started to dissipate when his phone buzzed in his pocket. Pulling it out, he glanced at the incoming call, and his sour mood returned with a vengeance. Dad. Ricky's sour mood deepened. He took a deep breath through his nose and blew it out slowly through his mouth before answering.

"Hey, Dad. What's up?"

"Hello, Richard. Just checking to see if you're still alive," came a gravelly voice over the phone. "It's been a while since you called."

"Sorry, I meant to, but I've been kind of busy." It was a lie. Ricky hadn't meant to call because he knew they would get into the same argument they always did and he didn't feel like fighting with his father.

"So, things are still going well for you out there?"

"Yes, sir. Just fine." Ricky kept one hand on the steering wheel and ran the other holding his phone over his forehead where a headache had sprung up at seeing his father's name on the caller ID.

A long pause ensued. "Do you think you'll be coming home anytime soon?"

"For a visit? Maybe over the holidays when things slow down at the ranch. We've got some cows due to calve in the fall, which is a pretty busy time."

An audible expiration of breath assaulted Ricky's ear. "I wasn't referring to a visit. You know what I'm talking about." Exasperation colored his father's tone.

Ricky gritted his teeth. "Dad, I *am* home. Wyoming is where I live now."

"Oh, Richard, how long is this pretense of playing cowboy going to go on? That's not who you are."

"It is now, Dad."

His father raised his voice. "Richard, for crying out loud, you have a PhD in physics. When are you going to come to your senses?"

Ricky closed his eyes and pushed down his anger. Forcing himself to speak softly, he replied, "Why can't you accept that this is what I want to do with my life?"

"Because you're running away from your life. You're ruining your life."

"It's still my choice."

"Richard, be reasonable. You were meant for better things than being a . . ." His father's voice trailed off as if he couldn't force himself to say the word.

"Cowboy? It's an honest profession, Dad."

His father huffed into the phone. "And what will you do when you're sixty? If you don't get established in your career now, you'll be way behind the curve. You had a good job lined up that you just flushed away. You can't possibly be making enough money to get anywhere."

Ricky remained silent while his father continued with his tirade. He could never make Dad see that he was already somewhere. He'd never be rich, but he'd be at peace.

His father finally wound down. "Look, son, your mom and I miss you."

"I miss you too, Dad. Why don't you and Mom come for a visit? You've never been here, and I'd love for you to see how beautiful this area is."

"I don't know. We'll talk about it."

It was always the same story. "I'll try to call more often, I promise. But please accept my decision, even though you don't agree with it."

"All right, talk to you later, son."

His father disconnected and Ricky sat holding the phone. He knew his parents wouldn't accept anything less than his returning to New York to begin a ladder-climbing career at Hallivac or Riggs/Brewster as a research analyst. The thought of spending his days bent over his computer in a windowless office or where, if he was lucky, he might have a window with a view of the snarled traffic several stories below, made his gut clench. Even the lab held no interest for him anymore.

Moving away from the academic life and all that went with it had been the best decision Ricky had ever made. How he loved the freedom of the wide-open spaces and the honest, back-breaking work that left him too tired to think. Nothing had ever given him the high he experienced when he had to outsmart or outpower the big black beasts in his charge, the animals who weren't appreciative of his efforts to keep them safe and healthy. He loved ranching. He loved the honest, earthy smell of the cattle and horses and the sweet smell of hay. He loved being outdoors, even in inclement weather. He loved the magnificent sunrises and sunsets that painted the sky in colors so spectacular that only God could have designed them. One couldn't enjoy those special moments in New York City where the horizon was lost in skyscrapers and smog. In the times when he could simply be still and experience a glorious sunset or a night filled with stars too numerous to imagine, he could almost feel God's presence surrounding and comforting him. But he didn't want to feel it. He was still angry with God.

Yet, if he were honest with himself, he had to admit that if God hadn't taken Lily, Ricky wouldn't be here in Wyoming trying to heal. He would be tucked away in New York City in the high-priced apartment he and Lily had applied for—the one they'd been so ecstatic about getting. He would go to work every day on the subway, jammed together with hundreds of other nameless passengers, and toil away in an office all day, riding home at night with another group of nameless people all trying to survive in the loneliness of being lost in the crowds. But being with Lily had made everything worth it. As long as he had her, the dream of climbing the corporate ladder had seemed like an adventure, the beginning of a whole new chapter in their lives. They would have it all—money, success, recognition, and their love. They were so close. But when Lily died, so did the dream. Everything he had worked for became meaningless, and the city threatened to strangle him, pulling him down into its dark abyss until there was nothing left of him.

Wyoming had been his salvation. He hadn't realized just how much until he had been able to breathe the clean air and break free of the invisible bonds that had tethered him to the city. He owed Ben for taking him on as a ranch hand when Ben's financial situation had been shaky. As it turned out, Ben had had to let some of the workers go when times got tough, but Ricky had been such a good worker that Ben had kept him in place of some of the men who had been there longer. Ricky always tried to do right by Ben in appreciation for all that Ben had done for him.

The ranch came into view, and Ricky realized just how true the words were he had spoken to his father. "I am home."

CHAPTER ELEVEN

"So, are you joining us for the hayride tonight?" Ben asked as he and Ricky finished treating the cattle for flies. Spraying the less-than-cooperative beasts had been a long, hot, exhausting job, and Ricky was glad to be done with it. It seemed as if as much spray got on them as on the animals. At least he wouldn't have to worry about fly bites for the rest of the day.

"I don't think so. I'm pretty beat." Ricky took off his hat and wiped his sweaty face against his shoulder. A mixture of something reminiscent of a smelly locker room mixed with insecticide assaulted his nostrils. "Besides, I'd have to go home and shower."

"There's plenty of time. Or you can shower here if you want."

Ricky always kept a couple of changes of clothes at the ranch, and he knew that Ben knew it.

"Come on. We're having a cook-out before it gets dark, and Kendra makes the best potato salad I've ever eaten."

Kendra again. "I don't like potato salad." It wasn't true, but he didn't want to talk about *her.* "Besides," he heard himself saying, despite his disinclination to discuss the woman, "she'll probably bring her boyfriend. I'd look out of place." Why those words had sneaked out of his mouth, he had no idea. He could have kicked himself.

Ben narrowed his eyes. "Boyfriend? I haven't heard anything about a boyfriend, and believe me, if there were one, Darcy would know."

"Well, Red was pretty chummy with some suave-looking dude the other day when I made my trip into town to the feed store."

Ben's lips twitched. "Really? What were they doing? Necking on the street?"

Ricky's mouth pressed into a thin line. "Going into the deli," he bit out, through gritted teeth. The accusation sounded ridiculous to his own ears. He could only imagine what Ben thought.

Ben laughed. "Gracious! Eating lunch? What *will* the wanton woman do next?"

Ricky's lips disappeared altogether as his jaw clenched. Ben had better stop right now before Ricky got madder. The problem was he really didn't know why he was mad, and that made him even more irritated.

"Okay," Ben said, "do whatever you want. The invitation stands." He nudged his horse into a trot and headed back to the stable, leaving Ricky in a cloud of dust wondering what had just transpired.

"Well, you certainly made a horse's patoot out of yourself," Ricky muttered aloud. Why couldn't he learn to keep his mouth shut when it came to Kendra?

When the evening grew increasingly later with no sign of Ricky, Kendra gave up hope that he would show up. Darcy had told her that Ben specifically invited Ricky, but when it didn't look like he was coming, she'd made the excuse that he'd told Ben he was tired after chasing down and spraying cattle all day. Kendra didn't know whether to be disappointed or relieved. When they'd chatted a few days ago, it seemed they'd had a connection, fragile though it was. But who knew? On one hand, the guy had acted like he wanted her company, yet on the other hand, he appeared closed off and determined to stay that way. Kendra couldn't figure him out, so why should she waste time trying? Still, she couldn't deny the growing attraction she had for the dark-haired, dark-eyed, moody cowboy. But attractions and feelings couldn't be trusted. Her recent experience with Darin, and others before him, had taught her that much. She was a poor judge of men, starting way back with Aaron.

The Sunday school class had descended on the ranch like a hoard of locusts over an hour ago, devouring most of the food. The pairings had become more overt. Darcy and Ben, of course, were newlyweds, and Molly and Tim had recently developed into an item. The other twosome in their group, Audrey and Bill, although not officially a couple, nevertheless hung together. Then there was her. Not that Kendra had any romantic designs toward any of the male members of their group, but seeing everyone paired up still made her feel left out. Sometimes she wished they could all go back to being just one big happy gang, like they had been until a few months ago. But she supposed it only natural that attractions would blossom in a mixed singles' class. After all, where else were Christian young people expected to find potential mates with similar values?

As the sun gradually slipped from the sky, coloring the clouds in soft pastels of pink, orange, and purple, Ben said, "If everybody's had enough to eat, we'd best get this show on the road. I'll let Cam know we're about ready."

"I'm stuffed," said Molly. "Tim will have to hoist me into the wagon."

"Who's going to hoist me?" he retorted.

Bill snatched another brownie and stuffed it into his mouth. "Okay," he said around a mouthful, "let's go."

Audrey smacked him playfully. "That's your fourth brownie."

Bill chewed and swallowed. "So, who appointed you the brownie police? It would be rude not to show appreciation for the hard work Darcy did in making dessert."

Darcy laughed. "Yeah, me and Betty Crocker. We're a good team."

Kendra began to clear the picnic table.

"Just leave all that," Darcy told her.

"I was thinking I could clean everything up while you all go on the hayride." Kendra averted her eyes as she grabbed an empty dish to carry to the kitchen.

"What? You'll do no such thing." Darcy placed her hand on Kendra's arm. "The dishes will keep. We want everyone to have fun."

Kendra's melancholy intensified, but she didn't want to spoil the evening for the rest of the group. Forcing a smile, she said, "All right." Still, she felt like a fifth wheel.

The rumble of a tractor sounded in the distance. In

a moment, Cam, Ben's other ranch hand appeared from behind the barn atop the big John Deere towing the hay wagon behind him, the odor of diesel fumes hanging in the air. Everyone cheered like a bunch of little kids at a carnival.

"I don't know when I last went on a hayride," said Molly, bobbing up and down, her arms flapping with excitement.

Tim moved out of her way. "Gotta watch those swinging arms of hers," he muttered. "A guy's likely to get a black eye."

"I have blankets for everyone," said Darcy, carrying a huge bundle from the barn. "It may get a little chilly when the sun goes down."

Bill waggled his eyebrows at Audrey, who shot him a stern look.

"We don't need a blanket. I'm gonna keep my bride nice and warm," said Ben, putting his arm around Darcy and pulling her close. Darcy's jaw dropped in mock indignation. Everyone laughed.

Kendra's smile felt pasted on until she caught a glimpse of headlights turning into the driveway. Then her heart skipped a beat. Was it him?

They all turned to watch Ricky's Ranger make its way to where they stood. As he climbed out of the truck, Ben made introductions. Ricky gave a brief nod to each person, but his eyes rested on Kendra.

"Did I miss the famous potato salad?" he asked.

She grinned. "I think there may be some left."

His eyes drifted to the hay wagon behind the tractor with Cam perched on top. "Look's like you're ready to head out. I guess I'll have to wait for that potato salad."

"I thought you didn't like potato salad," said Ben.

Ricky scowled at him. "I never said that."

"Yes, you . . . Maybe I heard you wrong." Ben shot him a confused look.

"Okay. Everybody hop in." Darcy thrust blankets at people as they climbed aboard the wagon, everyone talking and laughing.

Kendra hung back, waiting until everyone else had settled in before casting a glance at Ricky, who stood off to the side.

"After you," he said, extending his hand.

She smiled and took his hand, allowing him to assist her into the wagon, although she didn't need help. He popped the tailboard into place, then deftly swung himself up and plopped down into the straw at the back of the wagon, away from the others. He leaned against the backboard and drew up his knees, his hands resting between them. Kendra hesitated a second before gently maneuvering herself into a sitting position next to, but not too close to him.

"It's a little prickly," she said.

Cam twisted around. "Everybody good to go?" At the enthusiastic response, he started at a slow pace.

Ricky stuck a piece of straw between his teeth. "You may not believe this, but I've never been on a hayride."

Kendra turned and stared at him. "Seriously? Where did you grow up? Timbuktu?"

He expelled a soft breath. "New York City."

"What?" she cried. "You didn't tell me that the other day." Her outburst caused everyone's conversations to cease as their attention shifted to the two of them.

"I didn't get a chance."

"Didn't get a chance to what?" asked Ben.

"Did you know Ricky's from New York City?" Kendra said, her voice overly loud and sounding somewhat accusatory.

Ben and Darcy now gaped at Ricky as though she'd said he was from Mars.

"Why didn't you ever tell us?" asked Ben.

Ricky shrugged. "Never came up. Didn't think it mattered."

Ben chuckled. "I never would have guessed. You're a real urban cowboy, then."

Kendra continued to stare. "You're just full of surprises."

Ricky huffed. "I'm not the only one."

"What do you mean?" She narrowed her eyes.

He waited a moment before everyone resumed their conversations before saying in a soft voice, "You had a date with another Pretty Boy. I guess you didn't learn your lesson from the first one." His tone dripped with disapproval. Although he wanted to bite his tongue off, he'd simply been unable to hold back the words.

"What? What are you talking about?" Confusion with a twinge of annoyance rose in her chest. What exactly was he accusing her of?

"The other day. At the deli." His eyes fell short of meeting hers.

"At the . . . Oh, yeah. I thought I saw you outside the window." She smiled at the recollection. I waved, but you didn't see me."

"I saw you and the Pretty Boy on the sidewalk. He was helping you off with your sweater."

She swallowed a giggle. Was he jealous?

Interesting. "So, you think Wade is another Pretty Boy, huh?"

"Seems to be the type you go for," he muttered.

"And what type would that be?" She couldn't help needling him a bit.

He shrugged, his eyes still on his hands. "You know. Smooth, sophisticated, never-get-their hands-dirty kind of guys."

She raised her eyebrows. "Really? And how would you know what type of man I go for?"

He pulled his hat down lower on his forehead. "It's just the type I've seen you with, that's all."

The tips of her lips curled up in amusement. Mr. Urban Cowboy definitely had a chip on his shoulder over seeing her with Wade. "Why does it matter to you?"

He stayed quiet for a long moment. Then he pushed his hat back and raised his eyes to hers. "Look, Red, I guess it doesn't matter. I just don't want to see you get in another situation like with Pretty Boy Number One. Guys like that can be deceiving. All charm on the outside and rotten on the inside."

Red? Did he just call her *Red*? "Oh, I don't think you have to worry about Wade. His wife would kill him if he came home drunk."

Fury blazed in Ricky's eyes. "You're dating a married man?" he hissed.

Her hand flew to her mouth as she stifled a giggle. It would only upset him more if she laughed at him. Trying to reassemble her face into a semblance of normal, she said, "Ricky, Wade and I are colleagues at Blalock. He asked me to lunch to discuss business. We aren't in a relationship, for heaven's sake. Please give me more credit than that."

He squinted his eyes. "What kind of business?"

She shot him her most innocent look. "Dissecting cats."

He blinked. "Excuse me?"

"You heard me. Dissecting cats. Wade is the head of the biology lab. He's having trouble procuring fetal pigs for the dissection lab and he asked me what I thought about using cats."

"Pigs." Ricky stared at her as if not quite believing they were having this discussion.

"Yes, that's what we were discussing at lunch. Oh, and I did ask about Carmen—that's his wife—and their kids. Are you satisfied now that he didn't have any ulterior evil motives?"

Ricky scrubbed a hand over his face. "Just trying to look out for you, that's all."

"Thank you. I appreciate it." She refrained from spitting out a smarmy remark that she was more than capable of looking out for herself. But his less-than-subtle way of grilling her about a potential suitor flattered her. He *was* interested in her, and not just in a brotherly, protective way. It was on the tip of her tongue to ask if he thought her type of man was a tall, dark, handsome cowboy, but she decided it best not to go down that road. He was trying to save face, after all, and not doing such a good job of it. She didn't need to stir up a hornet's nest by teasing him any further.

Changing the subject, she said, "Look at the stars. I never get tired of the night sky here. You can see for miles."

CHAPTER TWELVE

Well, that was the second time today he'd made a horse's patoot out of himself. Red wasn't buying his "only looking out for your welfare" explanation. Hadn't Ben tried to tell him she wasn't seeing anybody? But then, Ben didn't know everything. Glad that his hat covered his burning ear tips, Ricky gratefully accepted her gracious change of subject.

"Yeah, me either. Looking at stars, I mean." Good grief what was the matter with him? He sounded like an incoherent dolt. Maybe he should just keep his mouth shut. He could hear the others' quiet conversations, but couldn't make out what they were saying over the noise of the tractor. Nor did he care to. If he joined in any other discussions, he was only likely to shove his foot further down his throat.

He leaned back and took in the shimmering stars against the velvety black sky. A half-moon rose high above the horizon, partially covered by a small cloud, giving it an ethereal glow. A sense of peace enveloped him, as it always did when he took in the vastness of the beauty of the night sky. Before moving to Wyoming, he'd never been particularly aware of the sky, day or night. Here, it was impossible not to notice the handiwork of God. *The handiwork of God*? Why had that thought popped into his head? He shifted a little, stretching out his long legs, as he chased the idea around in his mind. Well, it wasn't that he didn't believe in God. He did. He was just angry at God, that's all. If God really loved him and cared about his life, as he'd been raised to believe, why had He let Lily die? Romans 8:28 or not, Ricky couldn't see any good that had come out of her death. But even as he mulled the thought over in his head, he realized, once again, that her death had been the catalyst that brought him to Wyoming.

But what about Lily? They were young and in love and on the cusp of having it all after years of struggling. She didn't deserve to have her life cut short. She had everything to live for, didn't she? Didn't they? A part of him had died along with her, and he didn't think he could ever find his way out of the darkness to wholeness again. He couldn't resurrect the death in his own soul.

Lily's happy. She's with Me. She would want you to be happy, too. Whoa! Where had *that* idea come from? It seemed as though God had spoken to him in a voice of thunder, although no sound disturbed the peaceful rumbling of the tractor or the buzzing of the night insects. A shiver traveled through his body.

"It's getting a little chilly. Did you grab a blanket?"

Ricky jolted back to reality. He glanced over at Red—when had he started thinking of her as *Red*? She sat looking at him with what he could only describe as a mixture of concern and uncertainty. Well, of course, she would regard him with some wariness after he'd basically accused her of two-timing him with a colleague from work when he and she weren't even in a relationship. They barely knew each other, so why wouldn't she find it a bit weird that he'd reacted so strongly to her having lunch with a friend? He'd acted like a jealous boyfriend. Shoot, he *had* been jealous, if he were honest with himself. But what right did he have to be jealous? He'd made it perfectly clear to everyone, especially himself, that he had no interest in forming an attachment to another woman. His brain apparently hadn't gotten the message to his heart.

She scooted a little closer to him and opened up her blanket, inviting him in. He hesitated for a brief second before grabbing the other end of the blanket and pulling it over both of them. She shot him a shy smile. His pulse thudded in his ears at her nearness. They sat awkwardly huddled together, yet apart, as though bodily contact had to be avoided. He gradually eased his arm up over the back of the wagon behind, but not touching her shoulder. Then the tractor hit a bump, jostling the wagon and throwing her against him.

Struggling to regain her balance, she said, "Sorry. I seem to literally keep falling on you."

He chuckled and dared to draw his arm around her shoulder. "That's okay. I'm used to it when I'm around you."

She gave him a cautious glance as though she wanted to flee.

"If we sit close together, it won't hurt so much when you crash into me."

She released a one-syllable laugh and relaxed, leaning against him. Ricky assessed the feel of her body next to his. Her body exuded strength and sturdiness, much like her personality. Strong and solid, yet feminine. She fit comfortably under his arm, as though she belonged there. He pondered how natural it seemed to have her there. Contentment settled over him, and he didn't even worry about what the others might say or think. He didn't need to look around to know the other three couples had cozied up as well. The animated conversations had ceased, replaced only by the hum of the tractor.

They rode in companionable silence, the passing moments becoming more precious as he was loathe to see the evening end. At one point, another bump forced her head into his shoulder, and he gently held it there with the hand he had casually draped over her shoulder. Her soft curls brushed against his chin and the side of his face. A slight whiff of strawberries reached his nose, and he realized the sweet smell came from her hair. She must use a fruity shampoo. For a brief moment, he tried to remember the scent of Lily's cherry almond shampoo, but couldn't seem to conjure up the memory. He was somewhat surprised to find he felt no sadness from the inability to evoke the past. *Lily's happy. She's with Me.*

He gazed down at the top of the head of the woman resting against him. Could he let go of Lily? If the revelation that had spoken to his heart loud and clear tonight was any indication, then the answer had to be yes. But letting go of Lily and opening up his heart again to potential heartbreak was something else entirely. He didn't know if he would ever be able to do that.

CHAPTER THIRTEEN

The tractor pulled the wagon back to the barn, and the group piled out.

"I've got the firepit set up for toasting marshmallows," announced Ben.

"Great. That long ride and the night air made me hungry again," announced Tim.

"You're always hungry," said Molly. "And the way you eat, it's not fair that you're a bean pole."

Tim shrugged. "Can't help it. I have a high metabolic rate. It's my cross to bear."

"We should all be so cursed," Molly muttered.

"Yeah, Tim, I don't think anyone sympathizes with you," said Audrey. "I just *look* at food and gain weight."

"Then stop looking," said Tim.

Audrey pursed her lips. "It's my fault for choosing the wrong parents. I'm genetically flawed."

"That's okay, Audrey, I'll eat your s'mores for you. It's a sacrifice I'm willing to make for the sake of your waistline," said Tim.

"Thanks all the same, but Bill likes women with some meat on them, don't you, Bill?"

When Bill failed to respond, Audrey smacked him playfully.

"Ow!" he cried. "Why do you keep hitting me?"

Audrey glared at him.

Bill rubbed his shoulder, making an issue of his injury.

"Okay, everybody, before this situation escalates out of control, grab your blankets and head to the fire pit," said Darcy. "I'll get the makings for the s'mores."

Ricky and Kendra hung back. "You go ahead. I need to do something first," he told her.

"What do you have to do?"

"I have to feed a calf."

"Feed a calf?"

"Yes. We had to pull her from her mother because the cow has mastitis. We're treating the mastitis, but in the meantime, the calf has to be bottle-fed."

"You feed her with a bottle? Like a baby?" Maternal yearning surged through Kendra's veins.

"She *is* a baby. Just a bovine baby."

"I want to see her."

Ricky's unreadable gaze settled on her. "Really?"

Kendra felt a grin spread across her face as she nodded, a lock of hair falling over her eyes. She brushed it back and tucked it behind her ear.

"Okay, come on."

Kendra walked next to Ricky, matching her steps to his long strides as they headed to the barn. He stepped inside and switched on the lights, bathing the interior with dim yellow light. Musky odors from the animals inside mixed with the sweet, earthy scent of hay and feed hung in the closed air. A whiff of leather reached her awareness as she took in the surroundings.

"Where's the calf?"

"This way." Ricky walked over to a pen a few feet away where a forlorn little black animal stood alone. The minute it saw Ricky, it let out one long bawl and pushed its head into the gate.

Ricky laughed. "She's gotten used to me being the milkman. She must be hungry."

Kendra's heart melted at the sight of the baby. "How precious! How old is she?"

"Couple of weeks." He unlatched the gate and scratched the calf's head as she nudged him. "Come in here and keep her company while I fix her bottle."

Kendra hesitated.

"Come on, she won't hurt you."

"Okay, what do I do?" Kendra stepped hesitantly into the stall brushing past the calf who was determined not to let Ricky get away. Not ever having been this close to a cow before, albeit a small one, made her a little uneasy. What if the animal charged her or pinned her up against the wall? As small as the calf was, she still outweighed Kendra. Still, Ricky assured her the calf wouldn't hurt her, so she would have to trust him.

"Just scratch her head. Talk to her if you want."

Kendra forced down her apprehension as she edged closer to the animal. "Talk to her? What should I say?"

He chuckled again as he moved out of the pen. "I'm sure you'll think of something. You 'bout talked my ear off the first time I met you. Do the same with her."

She narrowed her eyes and shot him what she hoped was a scathing glare. Unfortunately, he had his back toward her as he went to fetch the bottle, so he couldn't see her withering look. Maybe he would feel the fiery darts her eyes projected.

"Very funny." Turning back to the animal, she stretched out a tentative hand and rubbed the soft head. "I must say you are the biggest two-week-old baby I've ever seen. In fact, you're the biggest baby of any age I've ever seen." A long dark tongue shot out of the calf's mouth and wrapped itself around her arm, catching her by surprise. "Oh!"

"What's wrong?" Ricky called from somewhere in the barn.

"She licked me." Kendra laughed. "Her tongue feels like sandpaper. Slobbery sandpaper." She wiped her arm against her jeans. "Okay, you, dinner's coming. Just hold your horses. Hah! I made a joke. Hold your horses, get it? You see, you're a cow and . . . Oh, never mind."

"What are you jabbering about?" Ricky asked, returning with a large bottle.

Kendra planted her hands on her hips. "You're the one who told me to talk to her."

"Telling her jokes? That's a first."

"It's okay, she didn't get it anyway," Kendra muttered. "Oh, my goodness. That's the biggest bottle I've ever seen."

He smiled. "You want to feed her?"

Excitement bubbled up in her at the offer, and Kendra felt as though she were a little girl at a county fair. Her face stretching into a broad grin, she said, "Can I? What do I have to do?"

"Just hold up the bottle. She'll do the rest."

Kendra took the huge bottle and turned it upside down, holding it out to the calf. The baby latched on with enthusiasm, guzzling greedily. "Oh my gosh, look at her go!" Kendra giggled. "This is so much fun. I can't believe you get to do this every day."

Ricky chuckled as he rested his elbows on the top rail of the pen. "Believe me, it isn't all fun and games. This is just one of the perks."

"In some ways I envy you. Your life is so uncomplicated." She struggled to keep a grip on the bottle as the insistent calf tugged harder.

Kendra glanced up at his silence. A sad smile creased his lips. "Did I say something wrong?"

He shook his head. "No. It's just . . . Well, let's just say my life hasn't always been uncomplicated. It's still complicated in many ways."

She forced her eyes back to the animal she was feeding. "I'm sorry. I guess we never really know what another person has been through. I don't want to pry, but I'm willing to listen."

His smile slipped from his face. "Maybe another time. Tonight's supposed to be fun, remember?"

She nodded. "Looks like this baby has about polished off this bottle. I sure hope we don't have to burp her."

He laughed, and she was glad the melancholy moment had passed. "Yep, just throw her up over your shoulder and pat her back."

Kendra handed the empty bottle back to him. "I think I'll leave that job to you. After all, you're the paid, professional cowboy."

"Fair enough. Come on, we'd best join the others before they eat all the s'mores." He held the gate for her as she exited, and they walked back to the door, where he flipped the light switch, returning the barn to darkness. He deposited the empty bottle in the outside sink.

"Wow, it gets really dark out here," she said, trying to adjust her eyes to the sudden loss of light.

"I should have brought a flashlight. Oh, well, I'll hang on to you so you don't fall and break your neck. Better yet, so you don't fall on me and break *my* neck."

He looped an arm around her waist before she could protest, but then again, she really didn't want to protest. It felt nice leaning against him like she had in the hay wagon. She reached up an arm and slid it around his waist. When he looked down at her with a smile, she said, "Extra safety precautions."

They made their way slowly back to the firepit, where everyone seemed to be having a good time. Bill had brought out his guitar, and people were singing along to the chords.

"Well, it's about time you two showed up," said Ben, when they took a seat on a blanket around the fire. "We were going to send out a search party."

"Red and I had to feed that calf," said Ricky. "I was scared to go into that dark barn all alone, so I made her come with me."

Knowing looks passed around the circle. "Sure glad she was there to protect you," said Tim. "I could have sent Molly if you needed extra help."

Ricky laughed. "Nope, we did just fine, but thanks for the offer."

Red? He had called her Red in front of everyone. Kendra was only glad that it was too dark for everyone to see how red his comment had made her heated cheeks.

CHAPTER FOURTEEN

Kendra yawned through another faculty meeting and tuned out most of the blather. This time, however, she didn't flirt with Darin across the table. In fact, she did her best to avoid eye contact with him at all. To his credit, he had pretty much left her alone after their disastrous date, which suited her fine. As far as she knew through the college grapevine, he hadn't asked anyone else out. Maybe he had learned a lesson, but she doubted it. Jerks like him never realized that they were jerks.

After the meeting, she found Darin waiting for her in the hall. Curiosity piqued her interest. He motioned for her to walk a few feet away from the door where they wouldn't be overheard.

"Wow, dropping that bomb about finances sure came out of nowhere," he said. "I thought maybe they were just making an excuse with my circumstance, but things must really be bad."

She wrinkled her brow. To be perfectly honest, she hadn't paid attention. "What do you mean?"

He gave her an exasperated huff. "Weren't you listening?"

"I try hard not to."

Darin rolled his eyes. "The college is in serious financial trouble."

She waved a dismissive hand. "Oh, that. They're always yapping about how we're in the red. After a while, nobody bothers to pay them any mind. It's like the boy who cried wolf."

He raised his eyebrows. "Then why are they eliminating my position?"

Kendra's senses suddenly went on alert. "What do you mean?"

"I was supposed to be here for a year. But after the first of the year, I'm losing my position."

While this news came as somewhat of a surprise, she wasn't particularly sorry to see him go. Maybe it wasn't so much about budget constraints as it was about his arrogance.

"It's no big deal, of course. I'll be glad to get back to Boston. But what about you?" He gazed at her with what she could almost imagine a sincere concern in his eyes.

"What about me?"

"What will you do if they let you go?"

She laughed. "I'm not too worried about that. I've been here a long time. Besides, like I said, they're always talking poor mouth."

"Maybe you should look over the budget reports," he said. "I'm not sure you're as secure as you think."

Kendra frowned. What did she know about budget reports? She taught biology, not accounting. She'd always left those pesky details to others more knowledgeable about financial matters. Wasn't that what they got paid the big bucks for? But maybe she should have paid closer attention. A tiny frisson of worry crept into her mind.

She sighed. "I will. I admit I've been remiss in not concerning myself with Blalock's financial position."

He touched her arm. "I do hope your job is secure," he said, then turned to go.

"Thanks. I appreciate it."

She stood for a moment wondering whether to be concerned or not. Then, squaring her shoulders and swallowing her pride, she re-entered the conference room where Dr. Cochran still gathered paperwork to stuff into his briefcase. Kendra had to grudgingly admit that while she found the old man tedious, he was still a good administrator. He didn't look up as she approached on the thick carpet that muffled her footsteps.

"Excuse me, Dr. Cochran."

He shoved the last of his paperwork into his briefcase and snapped it shut. "Yes?"

She didn't know quite how to confess that she hadn't been paying attention during the meeting. "I, um, wanted to ask you about what you covered on Blalock's financial status."

Dr. Cochran shot her an annoyed look. "What specifically did you not understand, Dr. Clark? I believe I made myself perfectly clear."

The familiar, irritating warmth spread upward from her neck. "Yes, sir. I guess I don't understand business as well as I should. When people start talking about statistics and numbers, I'm afraid I have difficulty following." *Besides the fact you drag everything out ad nauseam instead of just getting to the point.* "Without going into particulars, what exactly is the bottom line?"

The man huffed out an exasperated breath. "The bottom line, Dr. Clark, is if Blalock doesn't have a substantial increase in the number of fall semester students, or if we can't get state funding, we are in serious danger of having to shut our doors."

Her heart froze. How had she missed that important bit of information? She chided herself for blowing off these meetings and allowing herself to daydream instead of focusing on the agenda.

He set the briefcase he had been holding on the table and continued in an annoyed tone. "As a private college, although we do get some state funding, it simply isn't enough to sustain operation. We've been operating at a deficit for several years, despite my requests for additional funds. I have been unsuccessfully applying for federal assistance for the last couple of years, but there is only so much money to go around. Blalock is a small, relatively unimportant school in the big scheme of things."

"But we still have a good number of students," she protested.

"In the science department, yes. However, the enrollment in most of the other departments is way under the required minimums. We've tried to maintain, but it's simply not economically feasible."

She had been living in a vacuum. Did she not realize what went on outside her department? "What about raising tuition?"

"We can only raise tuition so much. One reason students prefer Blalock is its lower costs. If we raise tuition to the price of larger universities, they'll simply choose to go to other colleges where they can get more for their money."

More for their money. Students got a darned good education at Blalock—at least in the science department. "What can we do?"

He compressed his lips. "I believe I made myself clear on that point, as well. The administration is doing everything it can. We will have our fall semester as usual, but if something doesn't drastically change, there may not be a spring semester." He glanced at his watch. "Now if you'll excuse me, I have another meeting to get to." Snatching his briefcase, he strode from the room.

Fear surged through her veins as she stood alone in the conference room. If she lost her job, what would she do? Her whole life was here. She had tenure here. Only one college, in Jackson Hole, was within reasonable driving distance. No other school in the surrounding area would be close enough for her to commute. Perhaps she needed to dig out her old resume and update it. How could this be happening? She loved it here.

In a daze, Kendra wandered out of the administration building back across the small campus to the science department. As she entered her office, she could tell by the looks on the faces of the staff that news traveled fast. Nobody said anything as she slipped into her tiny office and booted up her computer. She brought up the latest financial report, which she knew Dr. Cochran had discussed in detail at the meeting—too much detail, which was why she always tuned him out. Sifting through several pages of numbers, she came away with no real understanding of what she was looking at. No wonder she swas confused. The many columns of numbers swam before her eyes with no real meaning. Next, she brought up her classes for the fall semester. As usual, she had several students already enrolled. She wished she could bring up enrollment for other classes, but she could only access her own.

Where was her old resume? She had to search for a while before locating it. She'd never thought she would ever need it again. It would take a lot of work to redo everything, but she didn't have time to start on that now. She had a class to teach in twenty minutes.

Ricky drove past Blalock College on the way home after another busy day at the ranch. He didn't know why he went in that direction instead of his usual way. Yes, he did, who was he kidding? Not even himself. Like a teenager trying to catch a glimpse of a crush, he hoped to see Red—like she would be standing on the sidewalk out front just waiting for him to drive by. A twinge of disappointment that she wasn't there made him shake his head at his foolishness.

Although he had tried to guard his heart, he'd enjoyed the hayride and being with her. And he got the distinct impression she had felt the same. She hadn't objected to allowing him to hold her close with his flimsy explanation that she wouldn't fall against him and hurt him if the wagon hit another bump. Of course, neither of them had bought that silly excuse. He didn't like feeling this adolescent way, but his wayward heart refused to listen to reason from his brain. But when the evening ended, he hadn't made any move toward asking to see her again. He didn't know if he was quite ready for that step.

He'd only just come to terms with God over Lily's death. The lightning bolt revelation from heaven the night of the hayride had left him reeling. Still, he didn't know if he could venture into romantic territory again. For one thing, he didn't know how. He had only dated one girl in high school, the girl who later became his wife. How was he supposed to act with another woman? He liked Red. He liked her a lot. But they didn't know each other all that well. They had no history together or shared experiences, other than the few times they'd been thrown together. But he felt drawn to her, and if he were honest, he *had* deliberately waited for her to return the punch bowl, putting himself directly in her path so he could talk with her. He guessed the hayride was the closest thing to a date that they had experienced. But it wasn't as though he had asked her out. They'd just been at the same event and paired up out of convenience, rather than being the only odd people in the group, which would have been even more awkward. But there had been no denying the feelings she stirred in him. Yet he hadn't asked for her number. He'd just said he had a nice time when the evening ended, and they had gone their separate ways.

He could ask Ben for her number, of course. But Ricky didn't want to do that. He hated the fact he couldn't seem to get her out of his mind. He also hated the fact his earlier impression of her as being too "good" for a simple cowboy like him was wrong. She was down-to-earth and genuine. Hadn't she said she envied his simple lifestyle? If only she knew. Ricky sighed. That was another thing. What would she think of him when she discovered he had given up a promising career as a physicist to become a cowboy? What would she think when she found out he'd been married?

The problem for the moment, however, was there seemed to be no way to put himself in her path again. Unless . . . Could he really do that? Could he step foot in church again, where he knew he would see her? Of course, that would be so obvious, it would be laughable. Was he willing to not only give God another chance but risk being the target of teasing? He'd never taken teasing well. Ricky drew in a deep breath as he considered the possibility of going back to church. It wouldn't be easy. He'd been out of church for so long, he wasn't sure he could go back. A sensation close to panic rushed over him at the thought. Then a long-forgotten Bible verse sprang to his mind. Something about God not giving us a spirit of fear. So where had the anxiety come from? Another Biblical truth hit him like a slap in the head. Fear didn't come from God. It came from the enemy. Well, Ricky would be darned if he'd let the enemy win.

CHAPTER FIFTEEN

Okay, the enemy was winning. Ricky's palms began to sweat as he pulled into the church parking lot. His heart thudded against his chest wall, and his throat tightened. He hadn't told anyone he was coming because he didn't want a big fuss. Besides, if he changed his mind at the last minute, nobody would be disappointed, or worse, nag him about his decision. He had arrived a little late on purpose. This way he could slip into the back unseen and "accidentally" run into Kendra after the service.

What a total junior-high plan! Did he really want to see the woman that badly? He sat in his truck debating whether he did or not. If he didn't go into the church, he was bound to run into her sooner or later somewhere else. After all, he had managed to cross paths with her several times in the past few weeks without even trying. But it had taken two years of living here before he even met her. Still, she was friends with Ben and Darcy, and she would undoubtedly be at the ranch from time to time. And the way Ben acted like a matchmaker in trying to get them together would certainly work in his favor. He didn't need to make a complete fool of himself by being so obvious.

"Ricky?"

Ricky jumped at the voice outside his window. Great, just great. It appeared Red was running late, too. He realized he was trapped and didn't have a choice now.

Her face lit up as he slowly exited the truck. "I'm so glad to see you. Ben has told me he's tried to get you to church many times."

Ricky rubbed the back of his neck. "Yeah, well, here I am."

He stood rooted to the spot, appraising her and liking what he saw. She wore a flattering lilac-colored, short-sleeved sweater and matching skirt that flared gracefully just below her knees. The soft colors contrasted with and complimented her flaming hair. A simple strand of pearls graced her neck. Two silver barrettes with pearl insets held her wild curls away from her face. Her feet sported strappy white sandals, and he noted bright pink nail polish on her toes, which for some reason, amused him. She appeared sweet and feminine, not at all like the rigid professional woman in her severe suit and spiked heels he had met on that first day at the ranch. He hoped his good jeans and cotton shirt would be acceptable attire for church. He didn't own any dress clothes anymore.

"We'd better get inside. The service has already started." She made a move toward the building, then turned back. "Are you coming?"

He took a deep breath. "Yeah, sure."

Walking next to her, he didn't know whether to feel relieved not to have to go in alone, or more conspicuous than ever by being with her. People might think they'd planned this. No one would believe they'd happened to run into each other in the parking lot. He didn't want people to get the wrong idea and think they were together. *So what if they do? Who cares?* But as he wrestled with the thought in his mind, he realized he wasn't ready for that yet. Definitely not ready for that.

"How come you're late?" he said to diffuse his nervousness.

"My alarm didn't go off. I'm usually awake early regardless, but I stayed up way too late last night redoing my resume."

A new twitch of unease hit him. "Resume? Why?"

She sighed and fixed her gaze on him. "The college is in financial difficulties. I may be out of a job after this semester."

He stopped walking. "What? How can that be? I mean, the college has been around forever, hasn't it?"

She nodded. "Yes, but enrollment is down, and costs are up."

He couldn't believe how this news upset him. "What will you do?"

She shrugged. "Nothing is definite yet. I'm just updating my resume in case I need it."

A gnawing loss for something he didn't even possess gripped him. "What are your options?"

Kendra blew out a breath. "Well, there's one college in Jackson Hole. Other than that, nothing practical in terms of commuting."

"Then that would mean moving?" He didn't want to hear her answer. The thought of her moving away when he was just starting to feel his way with her filled him with an ache he couldn't define.

She nodded. "As much as I would hate to have to

leave here, I might have no choice. And I just made tenure."

"I take it tenure is not transferable."

She compressed her lips. "Well, it depends on the college. But in most cases, they prefer to hire someone without tenure so they don't have to pay as much."

He didn't know what to say, so he remained silent.

"We'd better go in. We're good and late now." She turned and started walking briskly toward the door.

Ricky followed, not sure how these conflicting emotions swirling through his head would ever sort themselves out.

They slipped in the back and took seats in the last row. The worship leader was finishing up a congregational song, one Ricky had never heard. He felt like an intruder, an imposter. At one time, he'd believed his faith to be strong, but when tested by Lily's death, he discovered just how fragile it had been. He knew for certain God had gotten his attention the other night. He knew Lily's spirit dwelt in a better place. God's word spoke of each person's number of days being written down before their life began. Ricky still didn't believe it fair that God had only allotted Lily such a short number of days on earth. But, on the other hand, God had shown His goodness to Ricky in other ways, such as bringing him here and placing Kendra in his path.

In his path? Now, God might be taking her away from him, too. A sense of lostness worried his mind, making it difficult to concentrate on the message from the preacher. If Ricky wanted to explore where a relationship with Red might lead, he needed to stop straddling the fence and move forward. If she wasn't interested, at least he would know. Anything would be better than remaining in this limbo. He made up his mind right then that he would quit all this tiptoeing around his growing attraction to her and just lay everything on the line. Today. After church. Still, resolving the issue in his head and carrying the plan out in reality unnerved him. He bowed his head and sent up a silent prayer for God to help him as he took this uncertain, next step. Would God help him? After all, Ricky hadn't talked to God in a long time. It would serve him right if God left him to flounder on his own. The story of the prodigal son suddenly popped into his head, reminding him of the father's love for his wayward son. A sense of calm replaced his unease, and he tried to focus his attention on the preacher.

Instead, he focused on Red's nearness and the gentle scent of her floral perfume. He stole little glances at her when he didn't think she was looking, and a couple of times she caught his eye and smiled. Once, she reached over and squeezed his hand, causing his heart rate to accelerate. She apparently understood how difficult it was for him to come back to church after being away.

After the service, Ricky wanted to escape, but Kendra lingered, waiting for her friends to join them.

"Ricky! What a surprise!" cried Ben, wrapping Ricky in a hug that made him uncomfortable and slapping him on the back. "Why didn't you tell us you were coming, man?"

"Because I knew you'd react like this," Ricky muttered, disengaging himself from Ben's embrace. Heat rose in his ear tips, and he quickly covered them with his hat, even though they were still in church.

"It's wonderful to see you here," said Darcy, who thankfully refrained from hugging him. Her inquisitive eyes darted between him and Kendra.

Kendra laughed. "You can stop right now, Darcy. I was running late this morning, and I found Ricky sitting in his truck in the parking lot trying to decide whether to come in or not."

Ricky's ears flamed even hotter under his hat.

"Are you coming to Francine's?" asked Ben, referring to the restaurant the group usually went to after church.

Kendra shot him a questioning look, then her eyes softened in understanding. "Um, I've got a lot to do, so I really can't join you today."

Ricky worked hard to keep his jaw from dropping. She *got* it! The woman picked up on the fact he didn't want to be with a group of people today.

"How about you, Ricky?" asked Darcy.

He shook his head. "Nah, I'm good. Thanks anyway."

"Okay, but if you change your mind, we'll be at Francine's." They turned and headed to the parking lot, leaving Kendra and Ricky staring at each other.

"So," he finally said, "do you really have a lot to do, or can you take time for lunch?"

She grinned. "A girl's gotta eat, doesn't she?"

He grinned back. "As long as you don't eat too much. Cowboys don't make much money, you know."

"Don't worry, cowboy. This girl can pay her own way."

"Oh no. My dates don't pay their own way."

Her eyes widened. "Am I to understand this is a lunch date?"

His pulse quickened. He had taken the first step. "If you want it to be."

Her smile stretched across her face. "In that case, I accept. And I'll do my best not to injure you."

CHAPTER SIXTEEN

"**Bringing a girl** to a spaghetti restaurant on a first date is just plain wrong," said Kendra, as she slurped a dangling noodle into her mouth. "It's hard to eat like a lady."

Although this place wasn't La Traviata, she didn't seem to mind. "I won't hold your atrocious table manners against you," he said, reaching over with his napkin to wipe a smear of sauce from her chin.

She huffed. "You see? I need a bib." She attempted to wind another forkful of spaghetti but still came up with loose ends. "I never could do this."

He laughed and twirled a mound of spaghetti onto his fork, leaving no dangling pieces. "It's all in the wrist."

"I have a better trick." She cut her noodles into small sections and lifted them to her mouth.

"Cheater."

"I promised not to injure you. I didn't promise not to embarrass you," she said with a smug grin.

He looked around. "Well, they haven't kicked us out yet. How about a banana split for dessert?"

She chuckled. "No, thank you. I've made a big

enough mess of lunch." Kendra took another few bites, then pushed her plate away. "I'm generally a very neat person. You seem to bring out the worst in me."

"Should I take that as a compliment or an insult?"

She pondered a moment. "I suppose a compliment. For some reason, I'm a total klutz whenever you're around. You must make me nervous for some reason."

He raised his eyebrows. "I don't know why. I'm not a very threatening guy."

The delightful blush crept up her neck into her cheeks, and she lowered her lovely green eyes. "I guess because I find you attractive and I want to make a good impression," she said so softly he could barely hear.

His eyebrows rose into his hairline.

She raised her eyes and gave him a shy smile. "I haven't done such a great job of making a good impression."

"Oh, I don't know. You literally fell for me the day we met. That made quite an impression."

She laughed. "Falling *for* you and falling *on* you are two different things." Her expression became serious. "You're a nice guy, Ricky."

The tips of his ears warmed, and he reached up a hand to pull his hair over them. "Thanks. I try."

Her eyes locked on his. "But you're a mystery. You just appeared out of nowhere. Then I find out you're from New York City, of all things, and moved out here to become a cowboy. There's a story there. What's your story, Ricky?"

He drew in a shaky breath. If they were going to take things to the next level, he had to open up a little. A lump formed in his throat, and he tried to keep his voice steady. "I moved out here to start a new life after my wife died."

Shock and sympathy registered in her eyes. "You were married."

He nodded. "I haven't told anyone here. You're the first."

She licked her lips. "But why?"

Ricky looked down and became busy wadding up his napkin. "Because I couldn't bear to talk about it." His words came out raspy.

"I'm so sorry. I had no idea." She reached across the table and squeezed his hand. "You don't have to talk about it if you don't want to."

He swallowed. "No, it's okay." He raised his head and ran a hand through his hair.

She waited silently.

Ricky's gaze settled somewhere over her shoulder as he forced words past his thick throat. "Lily and I were high school sweethearts. We married after I graduated from college." His eyes briefly darted back to meet hers, and he saw surprise in them. His mouth turned up on one side in grim amusement. Yeah, she apparently hadn't figured him for a college graduate. He debated about telling her the rest of his education and decided not just yet.

"We lived in this crummy little apartment in not the best neighborhood." His mind drifted back to that run-down, tiny flat where they had lived on nothing but love. The past rose to meet him as clearly as though it were yesterday.

***

"Lily, I *have* to go to this reception tonight at the dean's house. I don't have any choice. How would it look for the new PhD. to not show up at a party being given in his honor?" Ricky stood before the mirror tying his tie. Lily sulked on the bed.

"But I told you I had to work tonight." She poked her lower lip out in a little girl pout.

He turned from the mirror, his eyes pleading with her. Ordinarily, he found her protruding lower lip adorable, but not tonight. "And I told you to call in sick since you wouldn't ask for the night off. You can go with me."

She looked away from him. "The invitation didn't include me."

He plopped down on the bed and put his arm around her, brushing her long blonde hair away from her face. "Lily, I'm sure it was an oversight. I told you that."

Her eyes filled with tears. "But you don't know for a fact it was an oversight. It might just be for faculty. I would feel out of place. Besides, we need the money."

He tilted her chin toward him and wiped the corners of her eyes with his thumb. "Forget the money. In another few weeks, we'll be fine."

She shook her head. "We still need enough to put the deposit on the new apartment. I don't want to lose it."

Ricky sighed. Their constant struggle for money neared the end, but they still had to get through a few more weeks. Right now, they needed every spare dollar to keep the option on the apartment.

He took her hands. "Honey, one night won't matter one way or the other. Call in sick."

She shook her head again. "Friday nights are the busiest. The tips are always good."

Ricky stood and ran his hand through his hair,

messing his careful combing job and eliciting a giggle from Lily.

"You always do that when you're upset." She stood and raked her fingers through his hair, patting the wayward strands back into place.

He caught her hands. "Promise me you'll have Pete walk you home. I don't want you walking home alone. I hate that I can't be there to pick you up tonight, but you'll probably be home before I am."

"I promise." She raised up on tiptoe and planted a peck on his lips. "Now get out of here. With the traffic, you'll be lucky to get out to the dean's house before the reception is over."

Ricky gave her one last hug. "Okay. I love you."

"Love you more."

He picked up his keys and paused by the door. "Two more weeks in this dump and we'll be living the good life."

"We already are." She blew him a kiss, and he headed out to make the long drive to Connecticut.

"That was the last time I saw her," he said softly.

Kendra waited quietly for him to tell her the rest.

"When I got home that night . . ." His voice caught, and he lowered his head, covering his face with his hands.

She reached across the table and placed her hand over his.

He drew in a shaky breath and said, "There were police everywhere. Lily was dead. The victim of a mugging gone wrong."

Kendra gasped. When he had first told her his wife had died, she thought it must have been from an illness or an accident. But murder? How did anyone survive something so horrible? Her heart hurt.

He raised his head, tears escaping from his eyes, and she wanted to wrap him in her arms and take away all the pain.

"They said . . ." He stopped, ran his hand under his eyes to brush away the tears, and swallowed hard. "The guy must have seen her put a lot of tip money in her pocket and followed her from the restaurant. He had a gun."

"Did they catch him?"

Ricky nodded. "Yeah. He claimed the gun went off by accident."

"I'm so sorry," she whispered. "What happened to the guy who was supposed to walk her home?"

"He called in sick."

"Couldn't she have taken a cab?" Kendra struggled to understand why a woman would walk alone late at night in a bad neighborhood.

Ricky shot her a look as though she were asking why Lily hadn't called for a spaceship. "You don't understand how poor we were. Besides, we only lived a few blocks from her work." He shook his head. "I almost always picked her up when she worked at night. If I couldn't, Pete walked her home."

"What a terrible ordeal. I don't know how you managed to get through such a tragedy."

Ricky dabbed his eyes with his napkin and took several deep breaths. "I couldn't. That's why I moved here. I think I told you I spent summers on my grandparents' ranch in Montana, and ranching gave me more peace than anything else I've ever done."

"I understand. This is the perfect place to heal."

She peered into his eyes. "You *are* healing, aren't you?"

He sighed. "I've taken things one day at a time. At least I'm not so angry at God anymore."

"That's why you refused to go to church?"

He nodded. "I'm working through it."

She smiled. "I'm glad. And I'm honored you trusted me with your history." She gripped his hand. "Thank you."

Ricky averted his eyes. "I figured if we were going to take things to the next level, I had to share some of my past."

Her heart skittered. "Are you saying what I think you're saying?"

He ran his hand through his hair, a habit she had discovered he did quite often, especially when nervous or frustrated. "Well, yeah, kind of."

"Kind of?"

He blew out a breath. "Well, you said you found me attractive and thought I was a nice guy."

She grinned. "Yes, I did say that."

He brought his eyes back to hers. "Well, then, except for the nice guy part, I guess the feeling's mutual."

"You guess?"

Ricky closed his eyes and took a long breath through his nose. "Okay, yes, the feeling's mutual." He opened his eyes and looked at her.

She wanted to laugh at his extreme awkwardness but knew that would forever close the door he had been brave enough to crack open. He had seemed so confident and capable in the past. She was only just beginning to see his vulnerability. "I'm glad we got that out of the way. Now what?"

He swallowed again. "Here's the thing. I don't know how to do this. I've only been with one woman since I was a teenager."

She grinned. "Don't worry. I'll go easy on you."

A broad smile stretched across his face, highlighting his gorgeous dimple. "No more physically assaulting me?"

"I'll do my best not to."

The smile slipped from his face as quickly as it had formed. He dropped his eyes again. "And you won't feel weird dating a guy who's only a cowboy?"

Her eyes narrowed. "Now you listen to me, Ricky. I am proud you want to date me. You're a good man, and that's all that counts."

"But the guys I've seen you with—"

"An arrogant drunk and a married colleague?"

He flattened his lips. "Professional men."

"So, you're saying you're not a professional man?"

"I'm a cowboy, Red. A ranch hand. Not exactly someone you'd want to parade around your faculty parties."

A sense of sadness washed over her. "Yeah, well, there may not be many faculty parties in my future if Blalock closes."

"One step at a time, Red. Don't borrow trouble from tomorrow."

She raised her eyebrows. "You're quoting Scripture to me now?"

"I'm not a total heathen. I've just been out of practice for the past couple of years."

She smiled. "We'll have to fix that. Come on, let's get out of here." Kendra stood and let him grab the bill, although she felt guilty about letting him pay. She doubted his paycheck equaled hers. But, then again, she might have no paycheck at all come January.

CHAPTER SEVENTEEN

Kendra's emotions bounced all over the place. She had finally met a man she dared to risk developing a relationship with. At the same time, her job could be in jeopardy, leaving her with no choice but to relocate just when her new relationship seemed to be taking root. Her inquiry at the college in Jackson Hole had turned up no employment prospect. How would she and Ricky fare in a long-distance relationship? Probably about as well as everyone else. Getting to know someone was difficult enough without miles separating them. Even if they became serious, at some point, he would have to move or she would have to find a different job if they wanted to be together.

Of course, that decision was a tad premature. But the possibility still had to be considered. She couldn't help but be concerned about the "what ifs." Asking Ricky to give up a job he loved wouldn't be fair. But she doubted they could live on his salary at Whispering Winds. Besides, she had to teach. She loved her job, and she was good at it. She could only hope Blalock's financial situation would turn around in the next few months.

"Dr. Clark, there's someone here to see you," came the disembodied voice of the department secretary over the intercom.

"Okay," Kendra said around a red pen stuck between her teeth. She had been correcting quizzes from her summer school students. "Send them in."

Thinking it must be one of her students, she bent her head back to her task, not bothering to look up when the door opened.

"What can I do for you?" she asked, laying down the red pen. When she finally raised her eyes, she gasped. "Oh my gosh! Aaron? Is it really you?"

The man who stood before her had aged gracefully, no longer the slim youth she remembered. His form had filled out into a man's strong body. His light brown hair, cut short, showed a touch of gray around the temples. But the eyes were the same. Sparkling green, like her own, as he gazed intently at her.

"It's been a long time, Kendy. You've only grown more beautiful."

She realized her mouth hung open and quickly closed it. "Wh . . . what are you doing here?"

Without being invited, he parked his behind on the corner of her desk. "I just moved back to town. I'm taking the job as the new football coach at the high school."

"Oh. That's . . ." That was what? A surprise? A sucker punch to her gut? Like seeing a ghost?

"So, how have you been?" His eyes continued to probe hers.

"Um, I'm fine." *Why are we having this ridiculous*

exchange of pleasantries when we haven't laid eyes on each other in ten years?

He looked around her cubicle. "It looks like you've done well for yourself. A professor. I'm impressed."

"Thank you." Somewhere in the dim recesses of her brain, she knew she should ask about him, but the words wouldn't move from her head to her tongue.

"You're not married?" His eyes returned to her, taking in her left hand.

"No. You?"

His mouth turned up in a sad smile. "Divorced."

She nodded as if his marital status explained everything, but it explained nothing.

"I've got two sons. My ex and I have joint custody, but she moved back to Cleveland, where she's originally from, so I doubt I'll get to see much of my boys."

Kendra blinked. Was she expected to respond to this revelation? She supposed she should offer some reply out of politeness. "I'm sorry to hear that."

He lowered his gaze and shook his head. "Yeah, me, too." Then, just as quickly, his head popped up and he flashed her a brilliant smile. "But I'm not here to talk about my problems. I want to know all about you."

Why? She spread her hands. "Well, you pretty much see everything there is to know. I teach biology. I've been here for ten years. I just made tenure."

His eyebrows rose. "No kidding? Congratulations. I always knew you were smart."

"Thanks." She didn't feel the need to enlighten him about her potential pending loss of employment.

He looked down at his hands. "Listen, Kendy, I've always regretted the way things ended between us. I admit everything was my fault. I was too immature and stupid to know what mattered."

She remained silent. He was right, after all.

"I just hope we can be friends. I'd like to get to know you again."

Glancing at her watch, she said, "I'm sure we'll be seeing each other around town. But if you'll excuse me, I need to go."

At that moment, Ricky stepped into the office. "Oh, sorry. Am I interrupting something?"

Kendra hopped out of her chair, grabbing her purse from the back of the seat. "No, no, I was just leaving."

Aaron rose, too, and the two men stood staring at each other. Kendra didn't bother to introduce them.

"It was nice to see you again, Aaron. Good luck with your new job." She hurried from the cubicle, Ricky trailing after her, leaving Aaron alone in her tiny work area.

"Who was that?" Ricky asked, as their footsteps echoed off the tile floor.

"Nobody," she growled, stomping through the corridor faster than she needed to.

"Whoa, wait up," he said, taking hold of her arm. "Obviously he's not nobody from the way you're reacting."

She stopped and heaved a sigh. "I'll tell you at lunch."

Once seated across from each other in the red vinyl seats at Vic's Bistro, Ricky waited until the waitress had filled their water glasses before revisiting the subject. "So, who is this man and why are you so upset?"

"My ex- fiancé, Aaron. He caught me off guard, that's all. I'm fine now." She busied herself with rearranging the salt and pepper shakers, aligning them with the silver napkin holder against the wall.

The revelation rocked him. "Fiancé? Why didn't you mention him when we were talking the other day?"

She dismissed the subject with a wave of her hand. "It was over ten years ago. I hardly ever give him a thought. I didn't think it was important."

Ricky stared at her. "I shared my deepest secret with you—one I've never shared with anyone else. And you didn't think it was important to mention the fact you were engaged?"

She tightened her lips. "He's been gone for ten years. I never thought I'd see him again."

Ricky snorted. "Yeah, well, here he is. Sitting on your desk as if you two are great, long-lost friends. As if those ten years apart didn't happen." He winced inwardly at the accusing tone of his voice.

Kendra's green eyes flashed with anger. "Don't start, Ricky. There is nothing between Aaron and me. He just appeared out of the blue today. It was a shock to me, too."

Ricky drew in a long breath, not wanting to appear jealous, but still needing to know where he stood in light of this new information. Did seeing her ex-fiancé rekindle feelings in her?

He made an effort to soften his tone. "What did he want?"

"He came by to tell me he's moved back to town. He's the new football coach at the high school." Her words came out clipped and curt.

The implications of this old flame moving back to

town caused the jealousy Ricky was trying to tamp down to flare up. "So where does this leave us?"

She jumped out of her seat and slapped her napkin down on the table. "It's going to leave us nowhere if you don't stop this irrational suspicion of every man I come in contact with."

He rose, too, feeling the rush of heat in his face. "I wouldn't call an ex- fiancé just any man." His raised voice carried through the small dining area, and several people turned to stare.

Her chest heaved as she glared at him. Finally, she said, "If you can't trust me, there is no hope for this relationship." She turned and practically ran from the restaurant.

I trust you. I just don't trust him. Ricky glanced around at the diners still taking in the drama. Mortified, he extracted his wallet and threw several bills on the table before following her out the door. He stepped out onto the street and looked both ways for her, but it seemed she had simply disappeared.

Had he blown it? Had he lost her before he even had her? Still, he didn't think he was being unreasonable, what with the reappearance of her old love. If Ricky had hopes of taking this fledgling relationship further, he needed to know how Aaron fit into the picture if, indeed, he fit at all. Ricky hadn't expected Red to get so defensive. Her reaction made him wonder just how deep her feelings ran for this guy.

Ricky didn't like this sensation of jealousy, something he'd never experienced in his life. But he wasn't going to fight for a woman's affections, no matter how much he liked her. He would not get caught up in drama. It figured. When he'd finally let his guard down and allowed a woman to slither into his heart, look what happened.

Running his hand through his hair, he berated himself for his foolishness. Never again. Slapping his hat on his head, he strode toward his truck. He wasn't cut out for the roller-coaster of dating someone new. He was better off alone.

Kendra peeked out from the alley running between the restaurant and the dry cleaners next door. She waited until Ricky had gotten in his truck and driven off before venturing out of her hiding place. Her thoughts rambled through her brain as she tried to sort them out. Shock at Aaron's unexpected visit. Anger at Ricky's reaction. Angry at herself for being angry with him. She had to admit Ricky had a right to know where he stood with her in light of the reappearance of her ex-fiancé. But his words and behavior had been unnecessarily accusatory, and she resented that. She remembered how Ricky had jumped to conclusions when she went to lunch with Wade. Was Ricky so insecure that he suspected ulterior motives in every man with whom she had contact? If so, this relationship was doomed before it ever started.

Perhaps the fight they'd just had was for the best. They'd hardly gotten off the ground with their new relationship, and with the possibility of her being out of a job in a few months, she wouldn't have to consider a relationship if she had to move. Besides, with everything so uncertain, this was a lousy time to begin something that would be impractical to continue in a few months. It was better not to invest more time and emotions in a relationship that had no future. She went back to her office to work on sending out more resumes.

CHAPTER EIGHTEEN

"Why are you in such a foul mood?" asked Ben as he and Ricky unloaded bags of feed from the truck.

"I'm not in a foul mood," Ricky snapped. "Jus' don't feel like talking."

Ben hefted a bag onto his shoulder and pegged Ricky with a piercing eye. "Does it have something to do with Kendra?"

Ricky slammed his bag onto the pile of other feed bags stacked in the barn. "There is no Kendra. We broke up."

"Broke up?" Ben set his bag down a little more gently than Ricky had. "What do you mean you broke up? I didn't know you were officially an item."

Ricky started back to the truck, but Ben caught his arm. "Hey, come on. I know you're upset. Talk to me, man."

Ricky shrugged off Ben's arm, but he made no move toward the truck. "Yeah, well, we were over before we really began. Her old fiancé is back in town."

Ben's eyebrows raised. "Aaron?"

"Yeah. He seemed very cozy in her office yesterday when I went by to pick her up for lunch."

Ben shook his head. "Wow, I had no idea. What's he doing here?"

Ricky scrunched his nose as though he smelled something offensive. "Moved back. Took a job as the football coach at the high school."

"Well, what did she have to say about him?"

Ricky shrugged. "Not much. She never bothered to tell me about him, and then, suddenly, there he was."

Ben sat on a hay bale and patted the one next to him. "Have a seat."

"We've still got half a truck-load of feed to stack." Ricky spun toward the truck.

"It'll wait. Take a break for a minute."

Ricky sighed and sank onto the hay bale, sitting with his elbows on his knees, his hands folded, his forehead resting against his fists.

"Look, boss, I'm not a touchy-feely type of guy. I'd just as soon put Red behind me and forget about it. We weren't meant to be."

Ben grinned. "You're still calling her 'Red.'"

Ricky blew out a frustrated breath. "Force of habit, okay? Look, I like her. I'm attracted to her, but as I told you before, we don't have anything in common. And I'm not going to compete with another man for her."

"Did she say she still had feelings for Aaron? It's been over ten years, after all."

"No." Ricky stared intently at the straw under his feet. "But it doesn't matter."

"Buddy, I'll be honest with you. I don't think Kendra was all that broken up when things didn't work out with Aaron. Remember, I was around during that time."

"So, what's the story?" Despite his words to the

contrary, Ricky was curious.

"They dated during the last two years of high school. But they went to different colleges. Even though they had an understanding of sorts, I don't think there was ever anything official. They grew apart. Kendra stayed faithful to him, but he didn't reciprocate. After college, he told her he wasn't ready to settle down. Then he moved out of state."

A slow burn began in Ricky's gut against the heel who had been Red's fiancé, or whatever he was. How could he lead her on for four years letting her think they had a future together? Ricky rubbed his hands across his face.

"I overreacted," he said.

Ben slapped him on the back. "Yeah, you've got to stop doing that."

Ricky rose and started for the truck again. "I'm just upset she didn't tell me about him."

Ben followed. "To play devil's advocate, you told me you'd just begun seeing her. She might not have gotten around to it yet. I sincerely doubt she withheld the information on purpose."

"Yeah, you're probably right. Now what do I do?"

"You got a big spoon?" Ben perched on the open tailgate.

"What?" Ricky's eyes narrowed.

"You've got to eat a lot of crow, buddy."

"Flowers? Seriously?" Kendra stood on her doorstep with one hand on her hip, one brow raised.

"Aren't flowers the accepted token of apology?" Ricky stood awkwardly holding the bouquet he'd picked up at the Piggly Wiggly in one hand and his hat in the other. What did he know about getting back into a woman's good graces? He'd been out of practice for too long. Besides, with Lily, he couldn't afford flowers, even from the supermarket.

"Not for this gal. You can't eat flowers. And they just die. Chocolate is the key to my heart, in case you ever need that tidbit of information for future reference."

"Oh, I should have brought chocolates, too." Why hadn't he thought about candy?

"Never mind." She snatched the offering from his hand and buried her nose in the center of the spray. "Mmm. Smells good. To what do I owe the token of an apology?"

She was not going to make this easy on him. "Aw, come on, Red, you know why. I acted like a jerk because you hadn't told me about Aaron."

She nodded. "Yes, you did." She managed to fold her arms over her chest with the bouquet dangling from one hand.

"Well?"

"Well, what?"

He ran his hand through his hair. "I'm sorry. Are you going to forgive me?" His tone lacked a certain degree of contrition.

She sighed. "I suppose since you put it so nicely. Come on in." She stood aside, allowing him to enter her small house.

It was the first time he'd been in her home. He glanced around at the attractive way in which she had managed to make the living room so inviting and cozy with an overstuffed brown sofa and armchair, Tiffany lamps on matching end tables, and colorful pillows tossed haphazardly. A moderate-sized entertainment center sat against the wall opposite the couch. The coffee table held an assortment of books, mostly biology textbooks, but he did spy a romance novel. The thought of practical, no-nonsense Red reading a romance novel tickled him for some reason. A black cat emerged from somewhere in the room beyond and wound its body through his legs, its loud purr rumbling in the uncomfortable silence in the room.

Kendra finally spoke. "Excuse me while I put these flowers in water. You can keep Seymour company."

Ricky bent and scratched the insistent feline behind the ears as it rubbed its face against his pants legs.

"I hope you're not allergic to cats," she called from the other room.

"No, no allergies."

He stepped gingerly away from the cat, who seemed bound and determined to trip him, and looked closer at several photographs gracing the wall. Her family, he guessed. He noticed, with a little degree of satisfaction, that she had no photos of Aaron displayed.

"Who are all the people in these pictures?"

She returned to the room bearing a mason jar in which she had arranged the flowers, and set it on a coaster on the coffee table. Seymour immediately hopped up onto the table and began to bat at the flowers.

"Seymour! Shoo!" She shoved the naughty cat off the table. "That's another reason I can't keep flowers. Seymour tears them up." She scooped the cat into her arms and moved over to where Ricky stood examining her photos. "Those are my parents and my brothers and sister."

"Nice looking family. I know your parents are in Florida, but where are your siblings?"

"Scattered to the four winds, I'm afraid. I'm the only one who stayed behind."

"Don't you miss them?"

"Yes, but this is home to me. My brothers joined the military and are stationed all over the globe. They're rarely in one place for more than a couple of years. My older sister married a man who got transferred to California. She hates it there, but she loves him. Such is life. I don't see nearly enough of my nieces and nephews." Kendra motioned toward the couch. "Have a seat."

Ricky settled onto the soft sofa and crossed his ankle over his knee, his hands clutching the rim of his hat.

"Would you like some coffee?"

"No, thanks, I'm good."

Kendra sat on the chair, Seymour in her lap, and leaned back. "Look, I'm mostly to blame for the scene the other day. I was so shaken up over seeing Aaron again, I'm afraid I took it out on you." She lowered her eyes and rubbed the cat's back.

"It's okay. I had no business prying."

Her eyes rose to meet his. "It's understandable you were concerned. You didn't know how Aaron's coming back to town after ten years would affect us."

"I have to admit the thought did give me pause to consider where I stood in your new-found affections."

A sad smile played around her lips. "You talk awfully smooth for a cowboy. But you don't have anything to worry about. Aaron and I were finished a long time ago. We dated in high school. We should have broken up when we went away to different colleges, but we were young and naive, and we believed our love, or whatever it was we felt for each other, would last for four years until we graduated and could get married. We didn't expect things to change, or that we would be two different people at the end of four years. Of course, our expectations were unrealistic." Seymour jumped down and hopped up next to Ricky, head-butting him. Kendra narrowed her eyes. "Traitorous beast."

Ricky scratched the cat's head again. "Who, Aaron or Seymour?"

She laughed. "Both, I guess."

"Didn't you see each other during those four years apart?" He stopped scratching, and Seymour nudged his hand with his nose.

"Oh, sure, during breaks and vacations. And sometimes one of us would drive to the other's college for the weekend. We were only four hours away from each other." She bent and straightened the flowers that Seymour had rearranged. "But I think I always knew, deep down, that we weren't right for each other. I just didn't want to admit it to myself because I was too caught up in fantasizing about getting married to consider the reality."

"I'm sorry your dream died."

"Don't be. It would have probably turned out to be a nightmare. Aaron told me he's divorced with two kids. That could be me."

Ricky nodded. "So, are we okay?" His eyes locked on hers for a fraction of a second before he looked away.

Kendra scooted over onto the couch next to him, earning her a protest from Seymour. She deftly removed the cat from next to Ricky and deposited him on the floor. "Yes, we are okay." She took his hand. "I'm sorry I didn't tell you about Aaron before. I wasn't deliberately keeping him from you. It's just that I rarely ever think about him."

Ricky's thumb played with the back of her hand, which felt so soft and small in his. He had a sudden urge to bring her hand to his lips, but he squelched it. "So, I need to know." He drew in a deep breath. "Is there any chance—"

She pressed her finger against his lips. "No. I have no feelings for him. I don't even know him anymore, nor do I care to."

The uncertainty in Ricky's mind vanished as her assurance filled him with peace. This time he didn't squelch his feelings. He leaned toward her and cupped her chin in his other hand. Then, slowly and deliberately, he brought his lips against hers. Sensations flooded through his body that he thought had died two years ago. He had never expected to feel this way again. He drew back and ran his thumb across her lower lip, gazing into those intense green eyes.

"Wow, you kiss pretty good for a cowboy," she said, pulling his mouth back to hers.

CHAPTER NINETEEN

Wow, his kisses! Kendra relived the way the sensation of Ricky's lips against hers made her pulse race and sent tingles through her body. She couldn't remember anyone's kisses affecting her so deeply. Of course, it had been a while. Until Darin, there had been no one to whom she had felt the tiniest bit of attraction. And, thanks to Darin's boorish behavior, the attraction died a quick death.

The kissing intensified until Ricky pulled back with a groan. "I'd better go," he whispered, his voice raspy, "before I forget I'm a gentleman."

With her own body ablaze, she had to rein in the temptation to take things further than they should go. She swallowed and moved away, somewhat embarrassed at her reaction.

He rose and moved slowly toward the door, as if reluctant to leave. She cleared her throat and followed him. Both stood for a moment by the closed door, as if not sure what to do next. He took hold of her arms and smiled down at her, his dark eyes dancing with joy.

"I think I'm falling in love with you, Red."

Her heart thudded against her ribs. Could this really be happening to her? After all this time?

"I kind of like you, too, cowboy," she teased.

"How about dinner tomorrow night?"

She didn't know if she could wait a whole day. "How about I make something here and you come over tonight?"

He hesitated. "Tell you what. You put together some sandwiches, and we'll have a picnic supper. We'll go to the Tetons and eat by one of the lakes. Maybe take a short hike."

"Okay, but can we go earlier in the afternoon? Before dinner?"

He laughed. "Woman, I have to work sometime today. I hope the boss hasn't fired me for being so late."

"If he does, I'll talk to the boss's wife."

Ricky gave her a peck on the lips. "I'll try to get off early." Placing his hat on his head, he opened the door and hustled down the walk. At his truck, he turned and gave her one last wave before climbing in.

She waved back, then closed the door and leaned against it, feeling a grin creep over her face. How would she get through the next several hours before seeing him again? She wished it wasn't Saturday so she'd at least have work to occupy her mind while passing the time. *Oh, Kendra, you've got it bad.*

Work! The thought sobered her as though someone had poured a bucket of ice water over her head. Before Ricky had shown up at her door, she'd been researching colleges with openings for professors of biology. She'd found a few and had emailed her resume. What would she do if Blalock folded? What would happen to her and Ricky? She couldn't think about that possibility right now—not with everything so perfect. The fall semester still lay ahead, and hopefully, Blalock's financial strain would ease by the time January rolled around.

She busied herself with cleaning and organizing, glancing at the clock every few minutes. Would these hours ever pass? Her head giddy with anticipation, she barely registered what she was doing until she found the dusting spray in the refrigerator. She gave up and pulled out sandwich fixings along with the spray. What kind of sandwiches did Ricky like? Kendra realized she had no idea. Did he like mayonnaise or mustard? Yellow or spicy mustard? White bread or wheat? She finally gave up trying to overthink the issue and made several ham and cheese sandwiches with different breads and condiments. Everyone liked ham and cheese, right?

Rummaging through the pantry, she found an unopened bag of chips and a box of shortbread cookies. She tossed everything into a picnic basket she dug out of the hall closet. She also located a small cooler that she filled with ice and several bottles of water.

At four o'clock, Ricky called and said Ben had let him off early. "I think he's trying to move things along between us," he said with a chuckle.

Bless Ben. He was such a good man. Kendra spent the next half hour deciding what to wear, settling on black jeans with a soft green sweater that brought out the green in her eyes. She had just finished trying to tame her curls when the doorbell rang.

"Wow, that was fast . . ." Her voice trailed off when she opened the door and saw it wasn't Ricky on her doorstep, but Aaron. "Aaron? What are you doing here?"

He shot her a charming smile. "I just wanted to

stop by and see how you were. Maybe catch up a little."

Panic rose in her chest. "I . . . I'm sorry, Aaron, but I've got plans. I'm just on my way out." *Please don't let Ricky drive up now. Please don't let Ricky drive up now.*

Aaron eyed the picket basket in the foyer, his hopeful expression changing to one of disappointment. "You're seeing someone."

"Yes." Her voice came out harsh in her distress.

He shook his head. "I should have known. That guy in your office the other day?"

Kendra's eyes did a quick sweep of the street looking for Ricky's truck. "Yes. Listen, we can talk another time, but I have to go."

Aaron made no move to leave. A sheepish smile played around his lips but didn't quite reach his eyes. "I should have known. I don't know why I expected to pick up where we left off, but I was kind of hoping we could reconnect."

"As friends, Aaron, but nothing more." *Please leave. Please!*

"Yes, of course." He bent forward and kissed her on the cheek. "It's great to see you again. You're more beautiful than you were ten years ago when I was too stupid to hang on to what I had."

Her hand rose to her burning cheek where his lips had touched her.

"Take care, Kendy." He turned and slowly made his way down her walkway to his car.

Kendra's heart skittered as she mentally urged him to hurry. When he finally pulled out of her driveway, she breathed a sigh of relief, her pulse gradually relaxing. No sooner had Aaron's car disappeared down the street than Ricky's truck turned into her driveway. She closed her eyes and took a deep breath.

He hopped from the truck and trotted to her open door, where she still stood, just inside the screen. He opened the screen door and planted a brief kiss on her lips. "Either you're really hungry or you couldn't wait to see me." His mouth turned up into the lopsided grin she loved.

Heat infused her face, and the irrational feeling of being caught in the act of something she shouldn't have been doing spread the heat to her extremities, making her light-headed.

"What's up, Red?" Ricky's sharp gaze locked onto her eyes.

"What do you mean?"

"Come on, you know your blush gives you away."

She turned away, reaching for the basket. She might as well be honest with him. It wasn't as if she had encouraged Aaron to show up. Besides, if they were to move forward, no secrets should come between them. "Aaron was just here."

Ricky's expression darkened. "Why?" He placed his hand over hers, taking the basket from her.

"He said he wanted to catch up." Her eyes sought his. "I told him I was seeing you. Please don't be angry."

Ricky sighed. "I'm not angry." He blew out a slow breath through his lips, then pulled her to him. "But if he doesn't leave my girl alone, I may have to punch him in the nose."

Kendra laughed. "You do realize that sounds terribly childish."

"I don't care. He had his chance and he blew it."

Ricky brushed the wild curls away from her face. "I want you all to myself. I'm funny that way."

She pushed away from his chest. "My gallant knight on his white horse. If it makes you feel any better, you have me all to yourself."

"It does. And for the record, the horse I usually ride is sorrel, not white."

"Whatever. Let's get out of here."

"Mmm, you make the best ham and cheese sandwiches." Ricky leaned back on the blanket they had spread out on the ground next to one of the many unnamed lakes in the park and closed his eyes, enjoying the soft warmth of the rapidly descending sun on his face.

Kendra laughed. "Thank you. Sandwiches are one of the few things I can manage without messing up."

Ricky couldn't remember ever feeling so content. At least not for a long, long time. Had God really given him a second chance at living again? He hadn't realized how he had trudged through the last two years dead in his soul until Kendra had managed to revive the small spark of an ember that hadn't quite died in his heart.

She nudged him. "Don't you fall asleep. We need to go for a hike to work off all the food we just ate."

He moaned. "I can't. I'm too full."

She poked him harder. "Come on before it gets dark."

With great difficulty, he opened his eyes. "Red, you're killing me."

"Come on, cowboy." She tugged on his arm. "Up."

"Remind me not to bring you flowers again," he grumbled, rising from his comfortable position on the ground.

"There's a trail just down the road. Let's see where it goes."

He picked up his hat and adjusted it on his head, then grabbed the picnic basket. "Better stash this back in the truck. We don't want to come back to bears."

"Good thinking."

Ricky placed the basket in the back seat of the truck. "Okay, Red, let's go. But no complaining if the trail gets rough."

She pointed to her sneakers. "I'll be fine. I left my stilettos at home."

He took her hand, grinning at the memory of her teetering across the barnyard in her ridiculous shoes the first day he'd met her, and they ambled down the road to the trailhead in companionable silence. They stopped to read the sign at the trail entrance.

"You see? It's an easy half-mile loop," she said. "I'll be fine."

Stepping into the shade on the dirt trail, the temperature suddenly dropped with the absence of the sun. Shards of light sifted through the dense canopy, but not enough to stave off the chill of the approaching evening. Kendra shivered as they moved deeper into the wooded area, and he pulled her against him.

"Come keep me warm, Red," he said. "I need your body heat."

She wrapped her arms around his waist. "We should have brought jackets."

"I have an idea to warm us up."

Kendra raised her head, a smirky smile on her lips, and Ricky lowered his mouth to hers, drinking in her sweetness. Heat surged through his body as he lingered, everything else around him disappearing as he became lost in her eager response. He wanted her so badly. It would be so easy to give in and let himself get carried away in the moment. With great restraint, he pulled back and rested his chin on top of her head, a soft groan escaping his lips. His heart pounded like a trapped animal trying to escape, and his pulse thrummed in his ears.

"What's wrong?" she murmured against his chest.

"Nothing." The word came out breathy as he tried to reel in his runaway raging hormones. "I . . . I think we'd better head back." It had been way too long since his pent-up passion had had a release.

He felt her nod. Without a word, they turned and made their way the short distance to the trailhead. When they re-emerged onto the road, magnificent pastels lit the dusky sky as the sun disappeared behind low-lying clouds toward the horizon. They walked back to the truck, both seemingly lost in their own thoughts.

Ricky opened her door and waited for her to settle in. He took his time getting around to his side, willing himself to gather his wits. He climbed in and sat for a moment, finally turning to her.

"Look, Red, I'm sorry. I . . . you . . . I don't want to lose control. But, well, it's been a while."

Color flooded her face, and she looked away from him. "For me, too."

He wondered what she meant, but did he really want to know? This wasn't the Victorian Age, after all, but still, she was a good Christian girl, wasn't she?

As if in answer to his unspoken question, she said, "I'm not perfect, Ricky. I've done things I regret."

Her truthfulness saddened him, but he was glad she

felt comfortable enough with him to share a bit of her past. He didn't need details.

"Red, I want you to know. It's not just lust. I do have feelings for you."

"I know," she whispered. "So do I. For you, I mean."

He sighed. "We need to take things slow. I apologize for letting my feelings override my good sense."

She swallowed and nodded. "Yes. If we are meant to be together, I want to do things right."

"So do I." He reached over and squeezed her hand, then started the engine.

CHAPTER TWENTY

In an attempt not to fall into temptation, Ricky and Kendra kept most of their encounters in a public setting. The weeks stretched out in a new and wonderful journey of truly getting to know each other and falling more deeply in love.

Only the nagging uncertainty of where her future lay marred the bliss of Kendra's joy. Three colleges had responded to her resume offering her a position, but the closest one was still four hours away. As the fall semester progressed, the outlook for Blalock College remained dismal. Other faculty members were preparing to jump ship and move on when the semester ended. Kendra's shaky hope that circumstances would change finally died, and she had to face the inevitable.

After meeting Ricky for lunch on his day off, Kendra led him back to a bench outside the administration building before heading back to work.

"We need to talk," she said. The rapidly defoliating trees left little buffer to the chilly October wind whipping through their bare branches, but Kendra needed the privacy to have this discussion.

"Uh-oh. 'We need to talk' is synonymous with

'something really bad is about to happen.'" Although Ricky shot her a teasing grin, his eyes were serious.

"I'm going to be out of a job after this semester," she said, plowing on without trying to soften the reality of what her words meant for their relationship.

Ricky stiffened. "You're sure?"

She nodded. "Yes. I have job offers from other colleges, but they are several hours away from here." Seeing no way around their predicament, she left the ball in his court.

He blew out a long breath and tipped his head back to the gray sky. "Where does that leave us?"

She stared at her hands clasped in her lap, wishing she'd brought gloves. "That's just it. I don't know. I'm sure you don't want to leave Ben, but long-distance relationships are difficult to sustain."

Ricky remained silent for a long time. Then, in a voice so soft she wasn't sure she'd heard correctly, he said, "You could marry me, Red."

Her heart skipped a beat, then began to flutter in an erratic rhythm. "Wh . . . what did you say?" She turned to him, her eyes wide.

"I said you could marry me." He gazed at her with such an intensity she could feel the heat burning through to her soul.

"But . . . We've only been dating a few months."

"So? I love you, Red. I want to be with you. What difference does it make how long we've been together?"

A buzz of confusion swirled through her brain. How could this solution possibly solve anything? She still had to work. Besides, she doubted his salary as a ranch hand would support the two of them.

"I can take care of you, Red," he said as if reading her thoughts.

She stared at him. "But I can't just stay at home and be a housewife. I *have* to work." A bitter gust of wind stung her cheeks, and she huddled deeper into her jacket.

"Why?" He reached over and pried her clenched hands apart, taking both of them in his own.

Despite the cold, his hands felt warm against hers, and she welcomed the sensation of his strength and stability. For one fleeting moment, the idea of a strong man to take care of her seemed like a dream come true. But she knew that fantasy wouldn't last long.

Grounding herself back into reality, she said, "Because that's who I am. I can't just throw away everything I've worked for."

"Marrying me would be throwing everything away?"

She tightened her lips. "Don't make this an 'either/or' decision. My career is important to me. How would you feel if I asked you to give up doing what you loved?"

He caressed her cold hands with his thumbs as the icy breeze blew her curls into her eyes. She extracted one hand and brushed them away.

"If that's what it takes to keep you in my life, I would."

She shook her head. "You would quit the job you love and move away from the place you love and start over somewhere else?"

"If I had to, yes. If it meant being with you, yes." His dark eyes locked on hers.

"I couldn't ask you to do that."

"I'm offering."

She looked away. "You would eventually resent me. Besides, it's too soon to be talking about marriage and major life changes. Let's see where the next couple of months take us."

He blew out a breath but didn't argue. Pulling her against him, they sat in silence until the cold became too uncomfortable. "I'd better let you get inside. Your nose is starting to look like Rudolph's."

The comment eased the tension in the air, and Kendra giggled. "The curse of red hair and pale skin." She disentangled herself from his warm body and stood shivering on the sidewalk. "Kiss me quick before our lips stick together."

He obliged, then walked her back to the administration building. She stood inside and rubbed her arms, trying to circulate some blood to her chilled bones, and watched him make his way to his truck parked by the curb. Taking a moment to collect her thoughts from the unexpected turn of the conversation, she leaned against the wall and drew in several deep breaths.

Marriage? She hadn't quite been expecting *that* suggestion. But with her job situation, their relationship seemed at an impasse unless one or both of them made a major life change. Still, jumping into marriage for the sake of hanging onto a potentially promising relationship seemed a bit premature. She loved Ricky, and he was a good man, but was she ready to make a lifelong commitment to him?

Even though they had been dating for a few months, there were still areas of his life that remained closed off to her. He rarely talked about his family back east, and when she tried to get him to open up about them, he just said things were complicated. She couldn't understand his reluctance to discuss the reasons why things were complicated. And besides the little he had initially shared with her about losing Lily, he had said very little about the relationship he'd had with his wife or his life before moving to Wyoming. She realized she didn't even know what he had done for a living before leaving New York. Not the way to start a marriage. If they were to consider entering into something as serious as marriage, she needed to know everything—good, bad, or otherwise.

Their relationship, thus far, had drifted along primarily on the endorphins of good feelings and chemistry. But a real life together required a deeper level of communication, with complete openness and honesty. Yet, he said he would be willing to give up his life here and move somewhere else with her. What did *that* say about his commitment? Perhaps he was thinking more with his hormones than his head. And as much as she yearned for a life partner, she did not want to rush into anything, no matter how idyllic everything seemed at the moment.

But what was she going to do about a job? She didn't want to leave Baker and start all over someplace new. Could she do something else for a living? What? She loved her small town, but the employment opportunities were mighty slim for a professional woman. She supposed she could always teach high school, but the thought of dealing with teenagers day in and day out made her head want to explode. Although some of her students were immature, most of them had at least developed a modicum of sense. She enjoyed teaching at the college level. She enjoyed working with students who had clear goals and worked to meet those goals. Sure, there were the ones who goofed off, but they were only wasting their own time and their (or, more likely), their parents' money. She didn't have to coddle them along to make sure they graduated.

Glancing at her watch, she saw she had spent way too long daydreaming. Her office hours started in five minutes, and she had a PowerPoint to set up for her three o'clock class. She dashed through the administration building and out the back to the science building behind it, relegating her tangled thoughts to a corner of her brain reserved for "later." Right now, she had to focus on her afternoon's work.

"I asked Red to marry me," Ricky said. He and Ben rode back from the pasture after their last check on the livestock for the day.

Ben swiveled in his saddle, his mouth open. "You did *what*?"

Ricky ducked his head. "I asked her to marry me."

"And?"

"She said it was too soon to be discussing marriage."

Ben huffed out an incredulous laugh. "I'd say she's right. You've only been together, what, two, three months?"

Ricky fixed his friend with a knowing gaze. "And how long was it for you and Darcy?"

"A little longer. But what's the rush?"

"She's going to lose her job at the end of the semester."

Ben's brows drew together into a frown. "Wow,

I'm sorry. What happened?"

"Blalock is in financial difficulties. They are ceasing to exist after the end of this term."

Ben blew out a low whistle. "I had no idea. How terrible for her. What's she going to do?"

Ricky took off his hat, ran his hand through his hair, and resettled the hat on his head. "She may have to move. There's nothing else around here. Unless I can convince her to marry me and stay here."

They rode along without talking, the only sound coming from the clop-clop of the horses' hooves and the crunching of dried leaves under their feet. A sharp wind rattled the few remaining leaves on the surrounding trees, sending several more floating to the ground and infusing the chilly air with the scent of fall.

Ben flipped his jacket collar up around his neck. He seemed to be weighing his words carefully. "Look, man, I know you like her, but do you think it's wise to try to keep her here when there's nothing for her to do?"

Ricky frowned. "I guess simply being my wife wouldn't be enough."

"Probably not for a woman like Kendra."

Ricky leveled his gaze at Ben, drew a deep breath of cold air into his lungs, and said, "Then I may have to move with her."

Ben stopped his horse and stared at him. "You're serious, man?"

Without his pulling on the reins, Ricky's horse stopped, too, seeming to sense the need to pause for this conversation. "I love her. I don't want to lose her."

Ben shook his head. "Look, I understand, but I think you're jumping ahead of yourself. You don't even know if she's taking a job somewhere else, let alone what opportunities there might be for you, wherever she ends up."

"I realize that. And it will be a while before anything is decided. I just wanted to alert you to the possibility."

The icy wind picked up even stronger, a harbinger of what they had to look forward to with the coming winter.

"Well, whatever you decide, I'll support you all the way, you know that. And it warms my heart to see you happy after what you've been through. I wish you'd leveled with me long before this, but I can see your need to hold your feelings close."

Ricky pulled his hat down lower over his ears. "Sorry, my history was hard to share. I didn't even understand, myself, how dead I was inside." A smile touched his lips. "But I sense God giving me another chance and I don't want to lose it."

"Let me give you some advice, my friend," Ben said, nudging his horse forward. "If Kendra is God's plan for you, the distance between you will not matter. He has a way of working things out."

"I know. I just wish sometimes He'd let me in on the plan."

"Don't we all?" Ben urged his horse to pick up the pace. "I don't know about you, but I'm ready to get out of this cold wind and into a warm house. Plus, Darcy's making lasagna tonight."

"Sounds good," said Ricky, stirring his horse to match the pace of Ben's.

"You're welcome to stay for dinner."

"Thanks, but I've got other plans."

Ben grinned at him before spurring his horse into a gallop back to the barn.

CHAPTER TWENTY-ONE

Winter hit southern Wyoming with a vengeance, dropping several feet of snow through November and December. Kendra tried to wrap up as much of her semester as possible before flying to Florida to spend Christmas with her family. She had a few administrative details to attend to when she came back, but before that, she had to figure out which job to take. She couldn't put the decision off any longer. Several colleges had offered her a position, and she needed to let them know before the first of the year. She had held out hope of something opening up in Jackson Hole, but nothing became available. With a heavy heart, she'd pretty much settled on Compton which, although the closest city to Baker, was still about four hours away. But the big city of Compton held little appeal. Having to take a pay cut along with losing her tenure also hurt, but thoughts of losing Ricky hurt more.

Her relationship with Ricky still hung in limbo. They'd both pointedly avoided discussing the future as the weeks leading up to Christmas flew by. He hadn't brought up marriage again, nor had he brought up moving with her. And, if she were completely honest with herself, as much as she wanted him to come with her, she knew it wouldn't be fair to him. He belonged here.

She planned to meet with a realtor when she came back from Florida to see about either selling or renting out her house. While she doubted she would ever return to Baker, the thought of selling the house she loved made her heart ache with a homesickness that had already begun to gnaw at her soul, despite the fact she hadn't left town yet.

After submitting the final grades to the office of the registrar, Kendra headed home to pack for her trip. With a sigh, she dug out her suitcase from her storage closet and began to sort through her clothes to take to Florida. She would miss Ricky and regretted not being able to spend Christmas with him, but she looked forward to a gentler climate and time with her family to clear her head. The break would be a good transition to her new life—a life in which she had to start all over making friends, colleagues, and contacts. She tried to push the depressing thoughts from her mind as she focused on happy times with her family. Her sister and her family were flying in from California, as well as one of her brothers, and she looked forward to the welcome distraction of the chaos with so many people under one roof again.

The ringing of her doorbell interrupted her rummaging through her closet to find lighter-weight clothing. She tossed a pair of capris on her bed and raced to the door, hoping it was Ricky. He had said he would stop by before she left.

Her heart did a little leap when she peeked out and

saw him standing on her doorstep holding a wrapped package. She swung the door open wide, a blast of cold air filling the foyer, and flew into his arms.

"I guess this means you'll be missing me," he said with a chuckle. He maneuvered them back into her warm house and closed the door to the raw cold.

Who was she kidding? How was she going to survive Christmas, let alone move away from this man for good? A dull ache settled in her gut as she rested her head against his chest.

He moved to the living room where he set the package down on the coffee table and lowered himself onto the couch, pulling her down next to him.

"My offer still stands to drive you to the airport tomorrow morning."

She shook her head. "If you do, I might not get on the plane."

"Would that be so bad?"

"Yes. My parents would kill me."

He smiled. "Well, we can't have that. I wish I could go with you, Red."

"Me, too." She wanted him to meet her family, but with all the commotion going on at her parents' house, it would be too overwhelming. He needed to meet her family gradually, not en masse. With their future unsettled, it would be too confusing, and she didn't want to answer questions later. Besides, Ben and Darcy were going to Darcy's parents' home in Pennsylvania for the holidays, and Ricky had to take care of the ranch.

He kissed the top of her head. "I'll miss you. It'll be awfully quiet around here."

They both avoided discussing the elephant in the

room as they snuggled together, lost in their own thoughts.

Finally, he spoke. "Open your present."

Her eyes moved toward the clumsily wrapped box sitting on the coffee table. "Did you wrap it yourself?"

"Is it that obvious?"

She smiled and reached for the package. "It's beautiful." She carefully removed the glittery paper to reveal a small, rectangular box. Pausing, she raised her eyes to his.

"Well, go on," he prodded.

After a moment of hesitation, she pulled off the lid. Nestled against a bed of cotton lay a thin gold chain with two entwined hearts. Fingering the delicate necklace, she whispered, "Oh, Ricky, it's stunning."

"This way our hearts will always be together. May I?" He reached for the necklace, and she handed it over, pulling back her hair. He leaned forward and fastened it around her neck.

Tears stung her eyes. "I don't know what to say."

"Say I can come with you," he breathed into her ear.

"What?" She swiped at a runaway tear and searched his dark eyes. "To Florida?"

"No. To wherever it is you'll be moving."

Her heart stuttered, and all sense of reason flew from her brain. "Okay."

"Okay?" He sat back and studied her. "Do you mean it?"

"Do *you* mean it? You won't regret giving up your life here?" She caressed the entwined hearts between her thumb and forefinger as her own heart filled with overflowing joy.

"I won't regret anything as long as my heart is with you."

Against everything screaming at her that this was not a good idea, she couldn't help the euphoria surging through her body, drowning out all the doubts and fears.

"I love you, Red. We'll start a new life together, wherever the road takes us." He enveloped her with his strong arms and claimed her lips with his.

She gave herself up to his embrace, lost in the pure bliss of his love.

CHAPTER TWENTY-TWO

With her heart back in Wyoming with Ricky, Kendra's time in Florida seemed unbearably long. She enjoyed the holidays with her family, but try as she might, she couldn't completely keep the yearning for him out of her thoughts.

"So, this cowboy, he must be something really special," said her sister, Tania. They sat cross-legged on Kendra's bed sharing "girl talk," reminiscent of the past when they had done so as children, and later as teenagers. At one point, Tania had not only been her sister, but her closest confidante, and Kendra had missed their closeness.

"He is." Kendra felt a sappy grin creep onto her face.

"I must say I'm surprised. A cowboy doesn't seem like your type."

Kendra raised her eyebrows. "And just what is my type?"

Tania shrugged. "I don't know. I guess I always pictured you with a stodgy professor puffing away on a pipe."

Kendra laughed. "Gee, thanks. Stodgy. Besides, I

don't like smoke."

"Well, I guess it's true opposites attract."

Kendra considered her sister's statement. "I wouldn't say we're exactly opposites. We're alike in all the important ways." But even as the words left her mouth, Kendra realized she was no closer to knowing the real man under the exterior dashing cowboy. They still hadn't delved into his past.

Tania hugged her. "I'm happy for you, sis. I hope all your dreams come true."

So did Kendra, despite the misgivings threatening to mar her happiness.

Kendra flew back home late in the evening, planning to head into her office the next day for perhaps the last time to tie up loose ends. She woke early, her body still on Eastern time, and gazed out the window to the gray sky and snow flurries swirling through the frosty air. Florida's sunshine seemed a million miles away. A lacy layer of ice clung to the edges of the outside glass, sending a shiver through her body. Only a few days away from Wyoming, and already her blood had thinned. She needed to readjust her internal thermostat.

After dressing in warm slacks, boots, and a double layer of sweaters, Kendra made coffee and poured it into her thermos before heading out to brave the elements. With her drive to the campus so short, the heater in the car didn't have time to dispel the chill, and she hurried into the nearly deserted science building, rubbing her gloved hands together.

A couple of other faculty members sat in their cubicles finishing their work at Blalock, the atmosphere around them quiet and cheerless. She nodded to them, asked briefly about their Christmas vacations, and settled down at her desk, a sense of nostalgia nearly overwhelming her. This place had been her second home for the past several years. Booting up her computer, she checked her messages and responded to one at Xavier College in Compton, where she had accepted the position of associate professor of biology. It was a step down, but better than being unemployed.

With her eyes focused on her monitor, she heard approaching footsteps but didn't realize they were leading to her cubicle until a man stood in her doorway and cleared his throat. She looked up at a vaguely familiar-looking gentleman who appeared to be in his middle sixties or so, an overcoat dusted with snow draped over his arm.

"Can I help you?" she asked, shoving her chair back.

"Dr. Clark?"

"Yes?"

"I'm Terrance Gaither, Richard's father."

After the initial shock, Kendra realized why the man looked familiar. Ricky bore a strong resemblance to his dad. She rose and held out her hand. "It's a pleasure to meet you, sir. Ricky didn't tell me you were coming."

"That's because I didn't tell him." He gripped her hand firmly as his dark eyes bore into hers. "May I?" He gestured to the chair just inside her doorway.

"Oh. Yes, of course." The man's presence rattled her, and she didn't know why. Although he and his son looked a lot alike, the older man's countenance seemed somewhat intimidating and cold. As he settled into the padded chair and looked around her tiny workspace, she said, "I don't understand. Why didn't you tell Ricky you were coming? I know he'll be thrilled to see you."

The man harumphed. "Well, I don't know about that. You see, Richard and I haven't seen eye-to-eye for the past couple of years."

Richard. That was the second time he had referred to his son as *Richard.* The formality spoke a hint as to why their relationship might be strained.

"How can I help you, Mr. Gaither?" she asked, sitting on the edge of her swivel chair, leaning forward and clasping her hands in her lap.

"First of all, I was surprised to hear that Richard was dating a professor. Pleasantly surprised."

She nodded, unsure of where the conversation was heading.

The man scrubbed a hand over his face, similar to the mannerism she had seen Ricky do when he was nervous. But other than that one small act, from all outward appearances, he seemed perfectly composed.

"Frankly, I was hoping you could help me talk sense into Richard."

She frowned. "I'm sorry, I don't understand."

Ricky's dad seemed to be searching for the right words. "Dr. Clark, with your educational and professional background, don't you find it odd that someone with a doctorate in physics would give up a promising career to play cowboy?"

The air rushed out of the room, and Kendra's heart plummeted into her stomach. Surely, she hadn't heard correctly. "Excuse me, what did you say?"

The man's eyes narrowed. "He didn't tell you." He pursed his lips.

Kendra struggled to draw a breath in the airless cubicle. "No. No, he didn't."

Mr. Gaither sighed. "I apologize for springing this news on you. I just assumed you knew." His eyes swept the ceiling before landing back on her. "After his wife died, Richard went off the deep end. He gave up everything he had ever worked for. Moved out here to start over, he said. His mother and I kept thinking this was just a grieving stage he was working through but, frankly, it's been long enough, and he needs to come back to reality."

She could do nothing but gape at the man. No words formed in her blank brain.

"I thought surely with your similar backgrounds, Richard would have discussed this with you." He sighed again and looked away. "But I see I've caught you completely off guard."

Kendra continued to stare at him, unable to fathom the implications of this revelation.

His entreating eyes landed on her again. "I was hoping you could help persuade him to give up this ridiculous fantasy of playing cowboy and get back into the academic world where he belongs. Richard has a brilliant mind."

Yes, he did. She had seen how intelligent he was.

"Richard tells me you're taking a professorship at Xavier College in Compton, and he's moving to Compton to be with you."

She swallowed around the tightness in her throat and nodded, not trusting herself to speak.

"I'm hoping this move will be a wake-up call for him. Could you, perhaps, inquire as to whether there may be an opening for a physics professor? Richard taught undergraduate physics while he worked on his doctorate. I know there aren't any research facilities near Compton, but he enjoyed teaching, and if there happens to be an opening, he might be persuaded to take it."

Mr. Gaither rose. "I've taken up enough of your time. I'm very happy to have met you, my dear, and I hope we can work together to get Richard back where he belongs."

She simply nodded again as she took his outstretched hand. When he had gone, she sank into her chair, her thoughts ricocheting through her head with a blinding force.

She had agreed, in a weak, lonely moment, to allow Ricky to come with her to Compton without addressing the issues that still lay unresolved—namely his reluctance to open up about his past. And what a past! Why hadn't he shared his background with her? Was he afraid she would try to force him back into his old life? Did he not trust her to understand his reason for abandoning his career to do something completely unrelated? Whatever, the simple fact was he had *not* told her. What else hadn't he told her? From the brief encounter with his father, she could tell Ricky had come from wealth and privilege. Why try to hide behind the facade of a simple cowboy?

Anger burned in her belly. How dare he pretend to be someone he wasn't! How dare he pretend to love her and yet not be completely honest with her! What kind of love was that? Relationships had to be built on trust, but he had not trusted her. She would not live with a lie, despite how attracted she was to him. She wasn't even sure who the man was she thought she loved. Bitter tears welled up in her eyes and spilled unchecked down her cheeks. How could she have been so foolish as to fall for a man she didn't even know? Well, she knew one thing. She was moving to Compton alone and swearing off men for the rest of her life. Never again would she let a man worm his way into her heart only to crush it.

CHAPTER TWENTY-THREE

"You had no right to tell Kendra about my past!" Ricky raged at his father.

"I'm sorry. I just naturally assumed you had discussed it with her." His father's face bore a look of confusion, but not necessarily penitence.

"Well, you assumed wrong." Ricky ran his hand through his hair as he paced the small living room of his apartment.

His father sat calmly on the well-worn sofa while Ricky continued to wear a path between the sofa and the front door. "I don't understand the secrecy. You say you love this woman enough to give up your job here and move to a strange city with her, yet you haven't told her about your background?"

"I had my reasons," Ricky bit out.

The older man sighed. "I won't pretend to fathom the reasons why you are being less than honest with the woman. But it seems to me this is a blessing in disguise. You may be able to go back to teaching."

Ricky whirled around to face his father. "I don't *want* to go back to teaching," he said through gritted teeth.

"Richard, be reasonable—"

"No, Dad, *you* be reasonable. That's not who I am anymore. That man died along with Lily. Why can't you understand that?"

His father shook his head.

Ricky grabbed his jacket off a peg by the door. "I need to go see Kendra. To try to fix this." Without waiting for a reply, he stormed out the door, hoping his father would be gone by the time he returned.

"I have nothing to say to you." Kendra stood in her doorway, her arms crossed over her chest, her chin lifted, and fire shooting from her angry eyes. Still, she didn't make a move to close the door.

"Please, just let me come in for one minute," he pleaded.

She pursed her lips. "You can say whatever it is in one minute right here."

"Red, come on—"

"Don't call me Red!" she snapped.

He held his hands out to his sides. "Okay, whatever you want, only please let me in."

Her chest heaved and her nostrils flared, the cold turning her hot breath to white vapor. "Fine," she said through clenched lips. She stood back, allowing him to enter, but stayed rooted in place.

Ricky edged his way into the foyer and closed the door behind him. "Could we at least sit down?"

"One minute. Say what you came to say and leave."

Ricky pulled a deep breath through his nose and blew it out slowly through his mouth. "Red, I'm sor—"

"I told you not to call me Red."

He closed his eyes, willing his words to be spoken in love and clarity.

Before he could begin, she exploded. "I cannot believe you withheld the fact you have a doctorate in physics from me all this time! Why? Why would you do such a thing?" She didn't wait for an answer. "But *you. . .you* went ballistic over the fact I hadn't gotten around to telling you about a relationship I had that was over ten years ago! What happened to openness and honesty?" She planted her fists on her hips.

"Red . . ." He stopped when her eyes shot poisoned darts at him. "Kendra, I don't know. I . . . It's hard for me to talk about the past because it opens up all the old wounds, and I can't bear the pain. It's like ripping off a scab and bleeding all over again."

Her eyes softened ever so slightly.

"I'm not the same man I was back then. That man and everything he was died with Lily."

She glanced away, but relaxed her hands, allowing them to dangle by her sides.

The silence between them seemed thunderous to his ears, but he dared not break it.

Still, without looking at him, she finally spoke. "I don't know who you are. I can't be with someone I don't know." She choked on her last words, and her eyes, which just a moment ago were filled with fire, now swam with unshed tears. "I can't be with you. I'm moving to Compton alone. We're through."

Panic rose in his chest, and he took a step toward her. She turned her back to him and lowered her head, her palm over her face.

"Please go."

He reached out a hand to touch her, then drew it

back. "Kendra, please, I'll do whatever it takes to make this right." He hated the hysteria rising in his voice, but he couldn't lose her.

"It's too late."

"No—"

"It's too late!" she yelled, spinning back to face him. "Go!"

He felt stinging tears as he stood for a long moment watching her tears sliding down her face. Then he opened the door and headed back into the cold, barely registering its bitterness. His heart felt icier than the brutal wind blasting from the outside.

"You're a *what*?" Ben's voice rose in disbelief.

"I said I had a doctorate in physics. I didn't say I was a physicist. I've never worked in that field. I'm a ranch hand." Ricky sat at Ben's kitchen table, grateful that Darcy was at work. He didn't have anyone else he could talk to and he needed to talk, but he didn't particularly want a crowd. Not that two was a crowd, but he felt more comfortable keeping the conversation just between him and Ben. He had come straight from Kendra's house hoping to find a friendly shoulder to cry on, and found Ben working on accounts in the farmhouse. Like the good friend he was, Ben had immediately put aside his books and invited Ricky in, putting on a pot of coffee.

Ben shook his head, then took a sip of his coffee. "Wow, you're full of surprises. I don't know what to say, man."

"Kendra doesn't want me to come with her. She says we're through. I guess, if you still want me, I can stick around." Ricky wrapped his hands around the warm mug of coffee in an attempt to stave off the chill that had settled in his bones, but the cold ran too deep.

Ben gazed at him with a look Ricky couldn't quite read. "You know you always have a place here. I'm just not sure why you want it when you could be making a lot more money doing what you went to school for."

"Because I left that life behind. Ranching is what brings me peace."

"But eventually you'll want to go back. You can't work that hard for something and then just walk away from it."

Ricky bit his lip. "I'm not that man anymore," he said quietly. "That was in a previous life." Why couldn't people see that?

Ben's gaze held his, but the message in his eyes was still unreadable. Finally, he said, "Give her some time. It's only natural she's upset right now, but she'll get over it after she's had a chance to think." He placed a hand on Ricky's shoulder. "Besides, Compton isn't that far away. A weekend visit might be more welcome after she's gotten a little homesick." A flicker of merriment passed through Ben's eyes.

Ricky nodded. "Thanks, man. I appreciate you being here for me." He scooted back his chair, the legs scraping across the wooden floor, and picked up his hat, turning to go.

"Any time."

As he let himself out the door from the warm kitchen into the frigid wintry air, he hoped Ben was right. He would give Kendra time and pray she'd find it in her heart to forgive him.

CHAPTER TWENTY-FOUR

Kendra had never been so homesick in her life. She disliked the big city, the sprawling campus, the traffic, the noise, and the large classes. The difference between the small-town atmosphere, where people knew and cared about each other, and here was like night and day. She hit the ground running, starting winter classes almost as soon as she arrived. Overwhelmed by having more than a hundred students versus twenty-five in her class made getting to know her students next to impossible.

Her co-workers were helpful enough, but mostly established, and some viewed her as outside competition, particularly since she had been tenured. The days seemed rushed and busy, with everyone concentrating on their own agendas, and having little time for interpersonal relationships.

Lonely and depressed, Kendra trudged home through the snow to the small apartment she'd rented just a few blocks from campus. With the traffic and the parking problems, it was usually easier to walk. Her boots crunched along the salted sidewalks as she bent into the bitter wind. The dreary sky, swollen with gray clouds that swallowed up the sun, made the short distance even more miserable. Ordinarily, a walk helped clear her mind and invigorated her, even a walk in the cold. But today, self-pity ran amok, scattering Kendra's thoughts. Was this what her life was to be from now on? No friends, no family, living in a place she didn't like, teaching at a college she didn't like?

She chided herself. It took time to get established in a new place. She would eventually find her niche, make some friends, and get into a new rhythm. Still, what was the point of trying? She hated it here. Her original reason for choosing Compton had been to stay as close as possible to Baker, to her old connections. She missed her comfortable little house. She missed her friends. She missed Blalock College. And she missed Ricky. But now, nothing mattered. On the discouraging trek home to her isolated little apartment, where she hadn't even met her neighbors, she made up her mind. She would fulfill her contract, but then consider moving to Florida, where she could at least be close to her parents.

With her head bent into the wind, the car horn blasting on her left barely registered. Then, as it persisted, she glanced toward the sound. The familiar face of a man bundled up in heavy winter clothing appeared through the open car window. She stopped in her tracks.

"Aaron?" She picked her way through the snow on the curb as the car pulled over.

"Hop in. It's too cold to be walking."

Stunned, she stood staring at him for a moment before moving around to the passenger side and slipping into the warm car. Pulling off her gloves, she held her raw hands in front of the blowing heater.

"I tried to catch you at the school before you left." He looked over his shoulder and eased back into traffic. "Where to?"

"I just live a few blocks from school. Turn left at the next light." She twisted in her seat to look at him. "What are you doing here?"

He shot her a smile before returning his attention to the congested road. "I'm headed to a conference upstate. I thought I'd stop in and see how you were doing."

Her inner warning system buzzed her brain. "That's nice of you, Aaron, but why?"

He put on his turn signal and merged into the left turning lane. "I thought you might enjoy a visit from an old friend."

Yes, she might, but not necessarily *him*. Still, he was here. She would have to display a modicum of hospitality. "My building is the third one on the right. Pull up behind the Suburban covered in snow. There's no extra parking for this building."

He did as directed. Switching off the engine, he turned to her, his expression expectant.

Stifling a sigh, Kendra said, "Come on in. The apartment's not much, but it's convenient for now."

He grinned and followed her as she struggled with the stubborn, frozen lock. She opened the door, divested herself of her satchel on a table just inside the foyer, and pulled off her knit hat, releasing a mass of red curls.

"Have a seat. Would you like something to drink? Some coffee or hot chocolate perhaps?"

"Just a bottle of water would be fine."

Kendra walked into the small kitchen and shoved her curls from her face as she opened the refrigerator and reached for a bottle of water. Turning, she jumped when she saw Aaron standing behind her.

"Sorry, I didn't mean to startle you." He gave her a charming grin and pulled out a kitchen chair.

She sank into the other chair and wrestled for something to say. The silence between them grew awkward until he finally released a long breath and said, "I heard you broke up with your boyfriend. I'm sorry."

Her lips flattened. "I'd rather not talk about it if you don't mind." Besides, she doubted Aaron's sincerity in being sorry about Ricky being gone from her life.

He nodded, the appropriate combination of understanding and sympathy in his expression. "Look, Kendy, my timing may not be the best, but . . . Well, I was kind of hoping you'd reconsider giving me another chance."

She closed her eyes and mentally counted to ten. As lonely as she was, renewing a relationship with Aaron did not sound appealing. He had burned her once. She didn't care to put herself in his line of fire again. She opened her eyes and cast a furtive glance in his direction. No lingering attraction or smoldering flame stirred her heart. The man was a stranger, one she didn't particularly want to know.

"I've always regretted letting you get away." He reached over and laid his hand atop hers, and it was all she could do to keep from snatching hers away.

She ran her tongue over her chapped lips and took a deep breath. "Aaron, I appreciate the thought, I really do. But we're two completely different people than we were ten years ago."

His eyes locked onto hers. "I know, but we have a history together. We can get to know each other again."

Her heart thudded with apprehension. "Aaron, even if I were so inclined—which I'm not—we live four hours apart."

"I'd be willing to move. I'm not locked into Baker."

Her jaw dropped, and she pulled her hand from under his. "That is totally irrational, Aaron. You just moved to Baker. You have connections there."

He regarded her with a sad smile. "One of those connections was you, Kendy."

She stood and leaned her hips against the sink. "Aaron, like I said, we don't even know each other anymore. Besides, I'm not looking to jump into another relationship."

He rose and gripped her arms, staring down intently into her eyes. "I won't push you. But I'd like the lines of communication to stay open between us. May I call you from time to time?"

What was she supposed to say? She pulled her eyes from his and focused on the wall behind his shoulder. "Yes, I suppose. But I'm not promising anything." Even if she were interested in rekindling the flame with Aaron, she had nothing left to bring to a relationship. Ricky had managed to kill any dreams for a romantic future, leaving her heart like a stone.

"Will you have dinner with me tonight?"

Exasperation rose in her chest. What about not pushing her? "I'm sorry, I have an evening class."

Disappointment registered on his face. "All right. I

can take a hint." He bent and kissed her cheek. "But I want you to know you can call me anytime for anything."

He started toward the door and she followed, relieved. "Thanks for coming, Aaron. It was nice of you."

Smiling, he stretched out his hand and tucked a lock of curls behind her ear. "I'll call you."

She mustered up a smile as he opened the door, then let it slide from her face the moment she shut it behind him.

"We thought we'd drive up for the weekend." Darcy's welcome voice warmed the chilly places in Kendra's heart.

"That would be nice. I'd love to see some friendly faces." She cradled the phone against her ear as she finished washing the last few dishes in the sink.

"Great. You can show us around, and we'll take you out for dinner."

"I'll happily accept the offer of dinner, but as far as showing you around, I'm afraid I haven't explored much beyond the campus and my neighborhood." Part of her desperately wanted to ask about Ricky, but she reminded herself that it didn't matter. They were finished. Still, she cared about him and his welfare.

"Aaron stopped by to see me on his way to a conference upstate," she said, trying to shift her thoughts away from Ricky.

"Aaron? Your ex-fiancé?" Surprise registered in Darcy's voice.

"Yes. He heard Ricky and I broke up."

Darcy's sigh carried through the receiver. "It's a

small town. Everybody knows everyone else's business. I'm assuming Aaron wants to renew a relationship?"

"Yes." Kendra wiped her wet hands on a dish towel and settled into a kitchen chair. "But I don't. I have no residual feelings for him. We were just kids. We didn't even know who *we* were, let alone how to move forward in an adult relationship with another person."

"Ricky will be glad to hear that."

At Ricky's name, Kendra stiffened. "What does *he* have to do with anything?"

After a long pause, Darcy said, "He's bound to hear Aaron came to see you."

"So what? I made it perfectly clear to Ricky that we're through. His deception was unforgivable."

"Kendra, I understand. You have every right to be upset, but in his defense—"

Anger stabbed at Kendra's gut. "He has no defense. He deliberately lied about who he was."

"He didn't lie. He's the same man he's always been, except he's more broken than ever right now."

Darcy's soft words hit Kendra with force, and she found it impossible not to allow a tiny crack to form in her heart. "Well, that's his own doing." She would not let the crack spread any further.

"Maybe so, but he lost himself when he lost his wife."

Kendra snorted. "Lots of people are widowed. But they don't lie about their pasts."

"Kendra, he didn't lie. He just walked away from the pain and tried not to look back."

Against her will, she began to see the reasons behind Ricky's omission. Some events were too devastating to revisit. Ricky had re-invented himself in a new life and couldn't bear to open the closed door for fear it would drag him down to depths from which he could not crawl free. She still didn't understand how abandoning his academic background fit into the decision to leave his former life behind, but perhaps his emotional stability was more fragile than it appeared on the surface. Outwardly, he looked strong and invincible. Inside, however, dwelt a crushed man who had just been on the verge of healing when she had dealt him another blow.

"You're right." Kendra sighed. "I should have been more understanding. Now what?"

"A phone call to him would be a good idea." The delight in Darcy's tone came through loud and clear.

Kendra smiled. "Okay." Her heart suddenly felt lighter as the heaviness from the past several weeks melted away. The tiny crack split through the icy barrier encasing her heart, leaving a puddle of warmth in her chest.

"Depending on how the conversation goes, I'm sure Ricky could be persuaded to join us this weekend."

Kendra's extremities tingled with hope for the first time in several weeks.

CHAPTER TWENTY-FIVE

Ricky couldn't believe his ears. Red was calling to apologize. At first, he thought he must be dreaming, but as Kendra poured out her soul and ended with a teary plea for forgiveness, he realized God had given him another chance. His throat thick with his unshed tears, he murmured, "I love you, Red."

"I love you, too. It doesn't matter what happened before. It only matters what happens now."

He pressed his head against the back of his chair and closed his eyes, waiting for his heart to stop racing with the joy of hearing her voice.

"Ricky? Are you there?"

He sat up and nodded, then remembered she couldn't see him. "Yeah, I'm here."

"You didn't say whether or not you forgive me."

He chuckled, the sound reverberating deep in his tight throat. "Oh, Red—can I call you Red again?—there's nothing to forgive. I was wrong not to share more of my past with you. It was just too painful to talk about. But that's no excuse. And I owe you an explan—"

"No, you don't need to explain anything."

Ricky drew in a shaky breath, his heart fluttering against his ribs. "No, I want to. I *need* to."

After a long pause, she said, "All right." Her hesitant tone spoke to her concern over probing into deep wounds.

He ran a hand through his hair. "I know you're wondering why I gave up academia."

"Well, yes, but—"

"Academia killed Lily," he said, his tone flat.

"*What*? What do you mean? I thought Lily was the victim of a mugging gone wrong."

Ricky pulled in a long breath and released it slowly, as he leaned his head back against the chair and closed his eyes once again. Every dark detail of that day and the ones that followed them flooded his memories as if suddenly released from a deep, evil abyss. For a moment, he sat frozen, unable to breathe, reminding himself this was why he'd kept a tight lid on that forbidden box.

He finally found his voice, although it sounded weak and thin. But that may just have been due to the thrumming of blood in his ears. "Academia was my life. I was absorbed in getting that degree and climbing the ladder of success. Lily didn't care all that much, but for me, it was all-consuming." He paused, as the last conversation he'd had with Lily played through his head like a bad movie. "I sacrificed a lot to finish my doctorate—time with Lily, time with family and friends, living in a run-down apartment in a bad neighborhood. I could have taken a good-paying job after getting my master's, but no, I had to reach the top, even if it meant living like paupers for years."

"What about your parents? Couldn't they help?"

Ricky huffed out a cheerless laugh. "They could, but I was too proud to ask for their help. They were not happy about Lily and me marrying so young, and they made it clear if we did so, we were on our own."

"I'm so sorry, Ricky."

"Don't be. It taught me self-reliance and strength and . . . pride, which was not such a good thing. All I could think about was getting that degree and finally being able to make a lot of money and live in a nice apartment and showing my parents I could make it without their help . . ." His voice trailed off. "We had a place lined up. We were set to move in two weeks."

Kendra remained quiet while he collected his thoughts.

"The night Lily died, there was a party at the dean's house honoring the PhDs. I *had* to go. It was expected—actually something between expected and ordered. I begged her to skip work and go with me, but her name was not on the invitation, so she felt excluded." He sighed, and his next words came out soft and full of regret. "I never noticed how uncomfortable Lily was around the academic environment. Or I didn't care to notice because I loved it so much."

"Why was she uncomfortable?"

Images of what he'd chosen to ignore flashed through his mind. "Lily never did all that well in school. I think, in retrospect, she felt like the people in my circle looked down on her because of her lack of higher education. It didn't matter a whit to me, but I think she felt snubbed, justified or not."

"She was a waitress, right?"

Ricky ran a hand over his face and swallowed against his dry throat. "Yeah, a darned good one. She largely supported us while I chased my dream. She was working that night because we needed the money for our new place."

"There's nothing wrong with that. Lots of people work and help put their spouses through school. The sacrifice benefits both of them."

He rose and grabbed a bottle of water from the refrigerator. Twisting off the top, he took a large swig and wiped his mouth on the back of his hand. "My almighty dream cost Lily her life." He sank back down into his chair.

"Ricky, that isn't logical. One thing had nothing to do with the other."

"Yeah, it did." His words came out bitter. "If I hadn't been so fired up about that stupid party, I would have been there to pick her up from work."

Her sigh whooshed in his ear. "Going to that party did not cause Lily's death."

"My wife should have come first," he moaned, his unshed tears now spilling over his lower lids and cascading down his cheeks. "I wasn't there for her, and I'll never forgive myself." He folded his arms on the table and collapsed against them, silent sobs racking his body. He was grateful Kendra couldn't see him.

"Ricky, you can't be with someone you love 24/7." A long pause ensued before she said, "If we decide to pursue a relationship, there will be plenty of times when we're apart. That's just life."

He tried to stifle his sobs but didn't trust himself to speak.

She continued. "You can't always protect the ones you love. You have to place them in God's hands. And even when things don't work out the way we want them to, we have to remember His ways are not our ways."

If she had spoken those words to him months ago, he would have ripped her up one side and down the other. Now, he understood the truth in them. Hadn't God spoken to his heart and told him Lily was with Him? That she was happy? Ricky hiccupped a couple of times and reached for a napkin to wipe his face.

"Ricky, you have to stop blaming yourself for something beyond your control. You had no way of knowing what would happen that night."

He released a ragged breath. "It's hard not to blame myself. If only—"

"We can't get sucked under with the 'if onlys.' You need to pray about it. If there was anything to forgive, God has already forgiven you. You need to forgive yourself. And academia."

He forced out a pitiful laugh. "I guess blaming academia is pretty silly."

She chuckled gently. "Sometimes we all have the need to blame someone or something else. But I think you can stop now. Especially if you want to date a college professor."

Despite the avalanche of feelings assuaging him, Ricky's lips turned up at the corners, and he realized his pain had dulled from its sharp, agonizing, paralyzing grip to a muffled ache. He had released the demons that held him captive to his fears, his sorrows, his regrets, and his blame. A light of hope dawned at the end of the very long, dark tunnel in which he had hidden himself for the past two-and-a-half years. He had opened the box of dark memories and emerged into victorious light, thanks to God and thanks to Red.

Despite their renewed connection, Kendra and Ricky decided to take things slowly. He didn't make any immediate plans to move, and she didn't encourage him to do so. With her dissatisfaction in her new environment, she doubted she would stay, so there was no reason for him to uproot his life to join her. They would cross that bridge another day. For now, she tried to take each day as it came.

They spent several weekends together, with one or the other of them driving back and forth, weather permitting. The miserable winter lingered, dumping foot after foot of snow, often making travel impossible. Kendra had never minded the winter before, but when it interfered with her limited time with the people she loved, she became frustrated. More than once, weekend plans had to be canceled due to weather.

After a couple of months, Kendra began toying with the idea of moving back to Baker when she'd fulfilled her contract. She didn't know what she would do to earn a living, but anything had to be better than staying in Compton when her heart remained in Baker. Fortunately, she'd kept her home, and it hadn't yet been rented, so she wasn't without options. She began researching jobs back home, but short of teaching high school, there was nothing in her field. She prayed for God to open the right door, and tried to be patient as she waited on His timing.

CHAPTER TWENTY-SIX

Ricky rested his arms atop the fence outside the barn, staring up at the star-filled night and wishing Red were here to share it with him. There was nothing so majestic as a clear night in the vast southern Wyoming sky, where a person could see for miles. He took in deep breaths of the clean, crisp air as white clouds of vapor escaping from his nose and mouth disappeared in the darkness surrounding him.

"I thought you'd left already." Ben's voice behind him interrupted Ricky's reverie.

Ricky turned toward his friend. "I'm going. I just got distracted by the beauty of the sky."

Ben's gaze followed Ricky's as he bent his head back. "God's handiwork. It's kind of hard to doubt the existence of a Creator when you look at something so immense and magnificent."

"Makes me feel connected to people I love and people I've lost, if that makes any sense."

"It makes perfect sense." Ben slapped him on the back. "Stay as long as you like. I'm heading to the house to warm up and grab some dinner. You're welcome to join me. Darcy's working late tonight, and

I'm on my own."

"Thanks, anyway. I need to be getting home." Ricky wanted to be sitting in his favorite recliner with his boots kicked off and a mug of hot chocolate in his hand when he had his nightly call with Red. Still, he couldn't help imagining the two of them in an open field on the ranch, snuggling together on a blanket, enjoying the wonder of the night sky. Maybe someday. It made him feel closer to her to think that she might be looking up at the same sky right that very minute. But that was probably foolish. If she had any sense, she'd be tucked away inside her cozy apartment, not out in the frigid night looking at the sky. Besides, in Compton, light pollution obliterated any view of the stars.

He kept hoping for something to open up for her here. He knew she desperately missed Baker and wanted to come home. Their time apart just made him miss her and long to be with her all the more. He looked forward to the next weekend when he would drive up to Compton if the weather cooperated and the snow stayed away.

Her semester would be over in another few weeks, then she would have a short summer break before returning for the summer session.

Kendra glanced at her watch and gasped. How had it gotten so late? She'd finished her evening class and headed back to her office to go over some papers. Somehow, time had gotten away from her. Ricky would be calling any minute. While she could talk in privacy here, she preferred to be home where she could relax, curled up on the couch wrapped in a warm blanket.

She stood and stretched, realizing how long she'd

been sitting in one position, oblivious to everything around her. Colleagues had not even poked their heads in to say good night, like at Blalock. She rolled her neck from side to side to work out the kinks from hunching over at her desk during the past couple of hours. Sudden awareness of being alone in the building filled her with a sense of disquiet. Chiding herself for being silly, she stuffed her laptop into its computer bag and slipped on her parka, zipping it up to her neck. The night would be especially cold without the sun to lessen the chill. She tucked her curls into her purple knit cap and wrapped her matching scarf around her neck before grabbing her purse and computer and making her way into the hall.

Her footsteps in the empty corridor seemed overly loud, and again, the creepiness of the empty building at night made her pulse quicken. She walked briskly to the exterior door, noting it was locked from the outside, and breathed a sigh of relief when she stepped out onto the icy sidewalk. *What is wrong with you? Why were you spooked by being alone in the locked science building at night? You were safer there than out on the street.* As if anybody in their right mind would be out on the street in this weather.

Her feet slid on the unsalted pavement, and she mentally cursed Mother Nature for plaguing them with more bad weather during the time she had been occupied inside the classroom, blissfully unaware of what transpired outside the walls of academia. There obviously hadn't been time for the maintenance crew to shovel and salt the walks. She wished she'd driven to the campus tonight, but driving conditions were often more hazardous and took longer than walking.

Reaching into her pockets, she dug out her gloves and wiggled her fingers into the tips. She picked her way carefully, trying to stick to the edges of the walkway where snow had piled up without leaving a treacherous layer of ice beneath.

Bending her head against the blustery wind, she crossed the street leading away from the campus. A figure stepped out from behind some tall bushes bordering the walkway on the other side. Kendra jumped, her already frazzled nerves causing her heart rate to spike, and her hand flew to her throat.

"Professor Clark?" The adolescent male voice came from a tall individual clothed from head to toe in black, with a knit face mask covering all but his eyes and mouth.

"Yes?" She tried to search the eyes of the person blocking her path, but his eyes darted all over like a trapped animal. He appeared agitated as if he didn't know what to do with his hands which seemed to be moving of their own volition. Alarm surged through her body as she realized the young man was apparently under the influence of something. Trying to remain calm, she said, "Is there something I can do for you?"

His mouth trembled under the mask. "I need to talk to you about my grade."

She stared at him for a moment before deciding to take an authoritative stand. "I will be happy to discuss your grade with you if you will make an appointment during my office hours," she said in her most professor-like voice. She attempted to step around him, but he moved, once again blocking her.

The young man shook his head, and she noted the tremors extended to his whole body. "No, I need to talk to you *now*."

Kendra took a deep breath through her nose, hoping her fear wasn't as outwardly evident to this disturbed student as it was on the inside. With her heart hammering against her ribs, she said, "This is hardly the time or place to discuss anything. I don't have access to my grades and I don't even know who you are."

His hands rose to cradle his head on either side. Whether it was an attempt to control the tremors or his anguish, she didn't know. She scanned the deserted street, hoping for a passing car or another pedestrian to appear, but they were completely alone. Muted streetlights cast eerie shadows over the darkened road while the snow banks lining the sidewalks rose in blinding stark contrast. Her hand delved into her pocket, digging for her cell phone. As her fingers curled around the phone, it suddenly began to play Ricky's ringtone, and she fumbled to pull it from her pocket.

As if unaware of the call, the young man shrieked, "I'm Eric Holbrook. How do you not know who I am when you've ruined my life?"

She glanced at the phone and quickly swiped the answer button, but didn't say anything. With several hundred students, she had no idea who Eric Holbrook was or what she'd done to ruin his life, but she surmised he probably had a failing grade due to lack of effort on his part. Ricky's disembodied voice floated into the night air. "Hello? Red? Are you there?"

Eric's eyes widened. "Who's that? Hang up!" He made a move as if to snatch the phone from her hand.

She nodded and took a step back. For a split second, she debated whether she could turn and run in the other direction, but quickly dismissed that idea. Her boots were slippery, and the boy, obviously ramped up on something, could easily overtake her.

"Okay." She held up her hand and turned down the volume button so Ricky could hear them, but they couldn't hear him. *Please, Ricky, call for help.*

Swallowing against her fear, she said, "Eric, suppose you tell me what this is all about?"

The boy made a strangled, anguished noise deep in his throat. "I can't flunk biology! I have to pass. Do you understand?" His hands squeezed against his head, skewing his face mask so she had a glimpse of a pointed chin sprouting a thin, dark goatee.

Willing herself to stay calm, she said, "If you'll come see me during office hours, I'll try to figure out what we can do to help you."

"No!" he shouted. "You have to change my grade. *Now*! Before midterm grades come out."

She had already turned in the midterm grades, but she wouldn't enlighten this deranged young man of that fact. *Tell him anything to get away.* "All right. I'll change it when I get back to the office."

His eyes narrowed. "I don't believe you."

"I promise."

"Change it now! Use your phone." He took a step toward her, and she shoved her phone into her pocket.

"I can't—"

"Yes, you can. All the profs have the gradebook app."

How did he know that? It didn't matter. She had to do whatever it took to satisfy him. Pulling her phone back out, she opened up the gradebook app and scrolled to his name, going through the motions of punching in data.

"All right. I changed your grade to a 'C.'" She started to return the phone to her pocket, but he moved with lightning speed and seized her arm, wrenching the phone from her hand.

With one hand still gripping her arm, he held the phone up, his wary eyes searching the screen. "What! You lied!" He threw her phone to the ground, where it hit the pavement with a sickening crack. "You already turned in the grades!"

Kendra shot one more desperate glance behind her, trying to decide what to do. When she turned around again, she came face-to-face with a gun.

"You lying . . ." A string of obscenities poured from his mouth.

"Eric, please. I'll fix this. I swear." *Lord, help me! I don't want to die like this*!

The gunshot split the still night air, filling it with a thunderous explosion. Kendra's eyes widened in disbelief before she crumpled to the ground, her body quickly numbing to the searing pain and cold. Her vision darkened, and the last thing she heard was Eric screeching before his running footfalls drifted farther and farther away.

CHAPTER TWENTY-SEVEN

"Kendra!" Ricky screamed into the phone. "Kendra! Answer me!" The noise that had blasted in his ear had to be a gunshot. While listening to the horrifying exchange between Kendra and some kid named Eric, Ricky's trembling fingers had been attempting to call 911. But in his panic, his efforts had been clumsy and unproductive, and he had only just now managed to reach the emergency operator.

"Please!" His words came out twisted and incoherent, and he had to force himself to slow down to relate the events as he heard them. He told the 911 operator what had taken place in Compton, hoping she could patch information over a statewide area. He didn't know how far 911 reached. Then, to be sure, he called directory assistance and asked to be connected to the police in Compton. Although he couldn't tell them which precinct, he figured it had to be the one serving the campus area.

After ending the call, he grabbed his jacket and keys and headed to his truck. He had to get to her. Blast it, why did she have to be four whole hours away? Why did she insist on walking to and from work? Just like

Lily. His heart stuttered at the thought. Images of Lily clouded his vision, and he brushed away tears he hadn't even realized he'd shed as he unlocked the truck and climbed in. He couldn't lose another woman he loved to a crazy gunman. Why was God letting this happen to him again? A desperate prayer formed on his lips, but if Kendra died, he didn't know if his faith would be strong enough to ever trust God again.

As he backed out of his parking place and slammed the gearshift into drive, he kept repeating, "Please, God, let her be okay." Despite the terror in his gut, a thought popped into his head. *If you trust God enough to put Kendra's life in His hands, you have to trust that His will is perfect.* A shiver ran down Ricky's spine, and he realized the thought had not come from himself. But he supposed he couldn't argue with the words. Besides, what else could he do? Everything was in God's hands anyway, despite man's best-laid plans.

"God," he whispered, "I hear you. Just . . ." Words failed him, but he knew God's Holy Spirit would intervene on his behalf.

Call your friends to pray. Yes. He needed to do that. He probably should have done so before rushing out into the night without the support of those who loved and cared about him and Kendra. The truck hit an icy patch and swerved, and Ricky made himself slow down. In his haste to get to Kendra, his foot had been heavy on the accelerator. He had four hours to go, and getting into an accident, himself, would do nobody any good. Easing up on the gas, he pushed the hands-free connection on his steering wheel to Ben's phone.

When Ben answered, Ricky tried to relate the sequence of events without breaking down. Hysteria would not help.

"Where are you?" Ben asked after Ricky told him what happened.

"Just getting on the highway." Ricky swallowed around the lump in his throat. "Would you call everyone and ask them to pray?"

"Of course. Then we'll be right behind you."

Ricky realized he probably should have asked Ben to drive him to Compton, or at least ride along with him, but he didn't want to waste any precious minutes. He hadn't been able to get to Lily in time. He *had* to get to Kendra. Even though he knew it was irrational, the thought that he could prevent Kendra from dying simply by being there took root in his mind, and he couldn't let it go.

Fortunately, traffic was light on the freeway this time of night and the road was clear of ice and snow. He set his cruise control at seventy so he wouldn't be tempted to speed, and drummed his fingers on the steering wheel as he willed the miles to pass. Then it occurred to him he didn't know what hospital Kendra would have been taken to. He wasn't familiar enough with Compton to know where the closest hospital to the campus was located, and he called Ben once more.

"We're just heading out," Ben told him, by way of answering the call. "I've called the prayer chain at church. Molly's waiting for Tim to get home from work and then they'll be heading up, too. Bill and Audrey are coming with them."

The love of his friends enveloped him like a warm blanket as Ricky grasped the depth of caring they had for him and Kendra. He wouldn't have to go through this ordeal alone like he had with Lily. He had been a loner far too long, and God had placed good friends directly in his path.

With his voice breaking, he said, "Could you do me a favor and try to find out which hospital Kendra's at? I can't do that and drive at the same time." He couldn't bring himself to call her "Red," as the lighthearted nickname didn't fit the seriousness of this situation.

"We're on it," he heard Darcy say. "You just concentrate on driving safely."

"I'm trying. I'm just so scared."

"We all are," said Ben, "but God's in control. And we're all here for you, buddy."

"Thanks." Ricky disconnected before his emotions got the better of him. He turned on the radio to try and distract himself from his fears, but the noise made the chaos in his head worse. Even the Christian radio station didn't help, so he turned the radio off.

Be still and know that I am God. Whoa! Where had *those* words come from? He knew they were Scripture, but the way they spoke directly to his heart had to be the not-so-subtle nudging of the Holy Spirit again. Sometimes a person couldn't hear the voice of God through all the noise of the world unless he remained completely quiet. If nothing else, God was speaking to him tonight, and he needed to listen.

One Bible verse after another having to do with the peace of God that passed all understanding danced across his mind as if spoken aloud, blending in a supernatural comfort. Ricky let the peace wash over him until his pulse and respirations steadied for the first time since he had heard the conversation between Kendra and that crazy kid.

He settled down for the rest of the long drive, filled with God's peace. Darcy called about halfway to Compton to tell him Kendra had been taken to Angel of Mercy Hospital close to the campus. The hospital wouldn't give her any other information over the phone. She had also called Kendra's parents in Florida, who were getting out on the first flight in the morning. She gave him directions to the hospital so he didn't have to punch them into his GPS.

Two hours later, Ricky pulled into the parking lot at Angel of Mercy and parked just outside the emergency entrance under a yellow light that dimly illuminated the largely deserted parking lot and cast indistinct shadows over the dark asphalt. Taking a deep breath, he shot one more prayer toward heaven, and got out of the truck, stretching his legs and back. He looked at his watch—not that he hadn't been acutely aware of the time flashing on his dashboard during the long ride. 3:15 a.m.

The automatic door to the emergency room opened with a swooshing sound, as warm air from the inside hit Ricky in the face and continued out to mingle with the bitter-cold air outside. He glanced around, noting with relief that the waiting room held only a couple of people. The hospital at night seemed strangely quiet. He made his way to the nurses' station, his steps echoing loudly on the polished floor. The people in the waiting room looked up, giving him no more than a passing glance.

"Um, excuse me, ma'am?" he said to the young nurse manning the front desk.

She directed her eyes away from the computer screen she had been staring at. "Yes, can I help you?"

He cleared his throat. "I'm checking on a patient who was brought in about four hours ago. Kendra Clark? She was shot." He couldn't believe how matter-of-factly he related the last detail.

The nurse squinted at him through oversized glasses and shoved the glasses up the bridge of her nose. "Are you a relative?"

"A friend. A *close* friend." Doggone it. He ran his hand through his hair. "I'm her boyfriend."

The nurse regarded him for a moment, then turned back to her computer. For a moment, he thought she'd dismissed him, but then she said, "She's still in surgery. If you'd like, I can show you the way to the surgery waiting room."

In surgery? Was that a good thing or a bad thing? He nodded and forced words past his thick throat. "Yes, thank you."

She motioned him through a door next to the desk and preceded him down the hall at a brisk clip.

"Um, can you tell me how she is doing?" he called to her quickly moving back.

"Sorry, I don't have that information," she said over her shoulder. She turned a corner, and he followed the sound of her squeaky sneakers as she disappeared from view around another corner. He caught up to her at a bank of elevators. "Take the elevator to the third floor. The surgery waiting room is to the right."

"Thanks." He tried to smile but feared his expression resembled more of a grimace.

"I hope your girlfriend is okay." Sincerity shone in her eyes, and he didn't trust himself to speak.

He nodded and stabbed the up button for the elevator. The helpful nurse retreated back the way she'd come.

The elevator took its time in coming, and Ricky tried to be patient. After all, he'd probably be waiting for a while. He found the surgical waiting room and opened the door. Not surprisingly, no other people waited for loved ones in surgery. He supposed middle-of-the-night surgeries were rare, involving true life-and-death emergencies.

Muted light from two table lamps lit the room, which was furnished with two comfortable-looking sofas and several padded chairs placed around three walls painted in a serene shade of blue. Neatly arranged magazines sat in the center of two coffee tables, and a mounted TV hung above the wall adjacent to the door. He spied the remote on one of the end tables, but he was just as glad the TV was off. The last thing he wanted was mindless noise. Besides, all hospitals and doctors' offices seemed to only feature home improvement shows, and he would rather wrangle the meanest bull on a bad day than watch those shows.

He sank onto one of the sofas and leaned forward, his elbows on his knees, his hands folded, feeling the need to continue praying. Exhaustion suddenly hit him in full force, but he knew he couldn't rest. His heart had simply uttered the same thing over and over during the hours on the road—*please, God.* Looking up, he spied a phone mounted on the wall next to the door, and he rose to examine it. A direct line into the operating suite could be reached by punching in the number two. He pressed the number and waited, holding his breath.

"O.R.," came a slightly gruff male voice.

"Uh, yes, I'm checking on Kendra Clark. She's in surgery."

"Hold on a minute." Through the receiver, footsteps sounded, then muffled voices, and finally the person Ricky had been talking to returned. "They're just finishing up. Someone will be out to talk to you shortly."

Ricky blew out the breath he had been holding. Finishing up was good, right? It meant she'd made it through surgery.

"Thanks," he said as he replaced the phone and laid his head against the wall. His pulse had accelerated again with the anticipation he would know something soon.

He wandered back to the sofa but couldn't sit still, so he paced the small area as the interminable minutes clicked by. At last, the door opened, catching him in mid-pace to the opposite side of the room.

He turned quickly to see an exhausted-looking, middle-aged man in wrinkled scrubs. The man reached up and tugged off his cap, revealing sweat-matted, dark hair plastered to his scalp. He ran his hand over his cheeks and lower jaw, which sported a five o'clock shadow. His bloodshot, puffy brown eyes locked onto Ricky's face, and even through the doctor's weariness, Ricky saw compassion.

"I'm Dr. Wright," the man said, extending his hand.

Ricky crossed the narrow space and grasped the doctor's hand in his cold, clammy one. "Ricky Gaither. I'm Kendra's boyfriend. How is she?"

The doctor sank into the nearest chair and motioned for Ricky to sit on the one next to him. "She's lucky. The bullet hit both her spleen and liver, and she lost a lot of blood. But we were able to patch things up and we didn't have to remove anything. Barring any complications, she should make a full recovery. But she's going to be out of commission for a while. We ended up having to do an open abdominal procedure. We tried laparoscopic first, but were unable to visualize everything."

Ricky closed his eyes, silent tears slipping from under his eyelids. *Thank you, Lord. Thank you.* Finding his voice, he said, "Thank you so much, Doctor Wright. When can I see her?"

"It'll be a while before she's out of post-op and in a room. Why don't you grab something to eat and get some rest? Even when she's in her room, she'll be heavily sedated."

"That's okay. I can still be with her."

The doctor rose. "All right. A nurse will come get you when she's settled. But it may be a couple of hours."

Ricky nodded. "I'll be here."

Dr. Wright gave him a tired smile and a squeeze on his shoulder, then took his leave. Ricky collapsed on the sofa, tears of relief continuing to flow, the hours of agonizing worry over.

He awoke when Ben and Darcy arrived. They wrapped him in a group hug and he updated them on Kendra's progress.

"Praise God," said Darcy, lifting her eyes toward heaven. "We haven't quit praying since you called."

Just then, a nurse entered. "Mr. Gaither, you may see Miss Clark now."

It was on the tip of his tongue to say, "*Dr.* Clark," but he pulled the words back. At this point, Kendra's title meant little. He looked at Ben and Darcy.

"I'm sorry, but only one person at a time may visit," said the nurse.

"It's fine. We'll be here," said Ben, taking a seat. Darcy joined him and smiled at Ricky.

Ricky nodded and followed the nurse down a long corridor to Kendra's room. As he entered, his heart swelled with a mixture of love and sorrow over seeing her lying so helpless, hooked up to all kinds of machines. He pulled up a chair and sat next to the bed, reaching for her hand without the IV. Bringing her limp hand to his lips, he kissed it, willing his own strength into her body.

Her eyelids fluttered open.

"I'm here, sweetheart. I'm right here."

"Ricky," she whispered. "Wha . . .?"

"Shh. You just rest. You're going to be fine."

"Don' know wha' happen." Her words slurred together as her eyelids lost their battle to remain open and drifted closed again.

"It's okay. Everything's going to be okay." He slipped her fingers between his.

In a moment, her even breathing indicated she'd lost the battle against sleep as well. Ricky's eyes drifted to the monitors as if he could keep her safe by ensuring all her organs were functioning normally—even if he didn't understand what all the numbers meant. But the reassuring blip of her steady heartbeat oscillating across the green ECG screen comforted him.

He didn't know how long he sat. He may have even dozed a little. But he became aware of thin slivers of light slipping around the edges of the closed Venetian blinds. He got up and went to the window, pulling back one side of the blinds. The sun hung low in the cloudless sky, a promise of a beautiful day. He looked at his watch. 7:40. Arching his back, he ran his hands along his lower lumbar area and massaged the knots that had formed during his stint in the hard chair.

Kendra hadn't awakened again. He really should give someone else a chance to see her, so he tiptoed out and headed back to the waiting area. As he opened the door, several people greeted him. Molly, Tim, Bill, and Audrey had all shown up, as well as a couple of people Ricky didn't know. The small room now swarmed with people.

"We got you breakfast," said Molly, thrusting a Styrofoam container at him after a long hug. "And don't you dare say you're not hungry. You *will* eat."

Ricky shot an amused look at Tim.

"Don't look at me," Tim said, holding out his hands in mock surrender. "She's the boss."

"And don't you forget it," Molly retorted, her hands on her hips and a smile tugging on the edges of her lips.

"Thanks, everybody." Ricky took the container and a thermos of coffee that Audrey handed him, and sat, grateful for a cushioned seat.

As he brought the thermos to his lips, he noted another familiar face across the room, but he couldn't quite place the guy. Then it dawned on him. Aaron! What was *he* doing here? Ricky set the food down and got up, anger rising in his chest.

"What are *you* doing here?" he growled through pinched lips, taking a step in Aaron's direction.

Ben positioned himself between the two men. "Hey, buddy, just take it easy."

Aaron raised red-rimmed eyes and gazed at Ricky,

but didn't reply.

"You *do* know Kendra and I are back together?" Ricky's question sounded more like a challenge. His hands balled into fists at his sides.

"I know." Defeat hung in Aaron's two words. "Doesn't mean I don't care about her."

Ricky took angry breaths through his nose, admonishing himself not to make a scene. That was the last thing Kendra needed. He allowed Ben to lead him back to his chair, but his appetite had suddenly vanished.

"You don't have to worry about Aaron." Ben lowered his voice so only the two of them could hear. "We had a long talk. He knows their relationship has been long over and Kendra is not interested in rekindling anything. She told him so."

Ricky's eyes searched his friend's. "She did? Really?"

Ben grinned. "Yeah, rather brutally from what Aaron said."

Ricky felt like a schmuck. Why did he always lead with his emotions instead of his common sense? He was going to have to work on that. Something else to pray about. But one thing he knew. He would do whatever it took not to lose Kendra again.

CHAPTER TWENTY-EIGHT
(Three months later)

Kendra sat on her patio sipping her early morning coffee and listening to the birds calling to each other through the dense thicket of trees along her fence line. She loved this time of year when everything came alive after the harshness of winter. In a way, she had come alive, too. The pain from the injury and the surgery lessened a little each day, although the emotional scars still ran deep. A therapist specializing in treating victims with post-traumatic stress disorder due to violent acts was helping her walk through the nightmare of coming to terms with what had happened to her. Little by little, she was healing.

It helped that Eric Holbrook had been apprehended shortly after the shooting and was facing attempted murder charges. His parents had given him an ultimatum of finishing college or being kicked out of the house. Although the young man had continually failed to apply himself, the sudden realization of being completely on his own caused him to snap. He would probably plead temporary insanity and beat the attempted murder charge, but Kendra couldn't obsess over what might happen. In a way, she almost felt sorry for the kid, but he still had to pay the price for his actions.

She had tendered her resignation to Xavier as soon as she was able to leave the hospital. The administration hadn't been happy about her breaking her contract, and they had made some posturing threats about legal repercussions, but in the end, they knew Kendra's medical condition prevented her from finishing the semester. She could also make a good case for being too traumatized to continue at Xavier.

Her parents had moved her back to Baker, and her mother stayed with her for a couple of weeks until she was able to get around by herself. Her parents fell in love with Ricky, who spent every free moment helping take care of her.

"I hear wedding bells for you two," her mother said, causing Kendra to blush and Ricky to chuckle and pull her close.

"She'll *have* to marry me so I can keep her out of trouble," he said.

Kendra snorted. "As if."

"Yes, I'm afraid you'll have your work cut out for you," agreed her mother.

Kendra smiled at the memory. She missed her parents when they left, but Ricky became her rock. Now she just had to figure out what she was going to do to earn a living. As tempting as taking on the job of becoming Mrs. Ricky Gaither sounded, she still needed to work.

"Red?"

Ricky's greeting interrupted her thoughts. "Out here," she called.

A moment later, his tall, lanky frame filled the doorway leading to the backyard. He held two Styrofoam cups in his hand. "I see I'm too late."

She set her mug on the metal table next to her chair. "Nope. A girl can never have too much coffee."

He leaned down and pecked her on the lips before handing her the cup.

She took a sip and sighed. "I hate to admit it, but this is better than the coffee I made. So, what brings you by so early?"

Ricky pulled his phone from his pocket. "I thought you should see this." He took a minute finding the site, then bent down to show her.

She scanned the information. "A STEM school? The county is transforming Blalock into a STEM school?"

"Yeah. I thought you might be interested. I know you said you didn't particularly want to teach high school, but this would be different. These kids are all the cream of the crop. They're all there because they've competed to be, so they're serious about learning." He settled on the cushion next to her as she re-read the posting.

"Hmm." She allowed the idea to take root in her mind.

He leaned toward her. "These kids are coming from all over the state. The campus will be full. And they're looking for qualified teachers."

"Hmm," she said again, as another idea came to her. "I'll make you a deal."

He grinned, but his eyes narrowed. "What kind of a deal? I thought this would be perfect for you."

"I agree. It sounds like an answer to a prayer. In

fact, it *is* an answer to a prayer."

"So, what's the problem?"

The corners of her mouth curled up. "I will if you will."

His brow furrowed in confusion. "If I will what?"

"Teach physics."

He sat back, throwing his hands up, palms outward. "Whoa! Hold on a minute. Who said anything about *me* teaching? This is an opportunity for *you*. I *have* a job. Remember?"

"You taught before. At the graduate level." She fixed him with a knowing stare.

He shook his head. "That was a long time ago. I wouldn't even know how—"

"Sure, you would." She scooted closer to him. "Come on, wouldn't you like to work together?"

He opened his mouth, then closed it again, a smirk forming on his face. "Sure. Are you saying you want to wrangle cattle with me?"

She pursed her lips. "You *know* what I mean. You could put your degree to good use and make a difference in the lives of young, budding scientists."

"I'm making a difference by providing them with beef."

"Ricky—"

"I'm happy with what I'm doing, Red." He stood and took his phone from her hand. "I need to get to work." He gave her a peck on the lips and started down the patio steps to the back gate.

She stood and followed him. "You wouldn't have to quit working at the ranch. You could teach part-time. Schools always need part-time teachers."

He continued through the gate without answering.

"Think how happy it would make your parents," she called after him.

He stopped and turned. "That was a low blow, Red."

She grinned. "Yeah, I know."

CHAPTER TWENTY-NINE
(Six months later)

In hindsight, perhaps a Christmas wedding had not been the best idea. With all the busyness of the season, not to mention unpredictable weather, they probably should have waited until school was out in June. But neither of them wanted to wait another six months, and the Christmas break was the only logical choice.

Fortunately, the snow had held off dumping the predicted ten inches, and the day had dawned sunny and clear. The roads and sidewalks had been cleared and salted from the previous snowfall a few days ago, making travel less worrisome. Kendra's parents had flown in the week before to help finish the final preparations for the wedding. They would celebrate Christmas with the newlyweds, then head back to Florida, where, as her mother put it, "We don't have to deal with this snow nonsense."

Kendra emerged from the shower to find her mother standing in the bedroom holding the phone. "It's your soon-to-be husband."

A prickle of alarm made Kendra's heart flutter. She took the phone her mother held out and cried, "Ricky? What's wrong?"

His warm laughter sounded in her ear. "Why do you naturally assume something is wrong?"

"Well, because . . ." She broke off, sputtering. "Why are you calling me? It's bad luck."

He laughed again. "It's bad luck to *see* the bride before the wedding. Not to talk to her. Don't worry, I don't have you on video."

"Oh. Okay. So? You're not having second thoughts, are you?"

"Hardly. Just making sure *you're* going to show up. Besides, I couldn't wait until four o'clock to talk to you."

She let out a relieved breath and smiled. "I'll be there. I'll be the one wearing white."

"Love you, Red. Can't wait to marry you."

"Me too," she said softly. She pushed the end button and laid the phone on her dresser.

"Everything okay?" asked her mother.

"Everything's fine. Everything's perfect." She couldn't help the sappy grin she felt creeping over her face.

Her mother hugged her. "I'm so happy for you, honey. You got a good man."

"Thanks, Mom. I was beginning to think love would never happen for me." *Always a bridesmaid, never a bride.* The words that had run through her head the day she met Ricky sprang to mind, and she had to laugh at herself. Who would have ever thought that the aloof cowboy—correction, professor/cowboy— would turn out to be her Prince Charming? Ricky had taken a part-time teaching job at the STEM school and found he loved being back in academia. Although he equally loved working the ranch, he and Kendra enjoyed the time together at the school.

"Some things are worth waiting for," said her mother.

"True. Only God could have brought two such unlikely people together," said Kendra.

"You are more alike than you realize." Her mother gave her a knowing look.

Her father poked his head into the room. "You're not even dressed yet! We're supposed to leave for the church in twenty minutes."

Kendra rolled her eyes. "We have plenty of time, Dad. Besides, it takes time for a girl to get ready on her wedding day. You want me to look good, don't you?"

He crossed the room and took hold of her arms, his eyes shining down at her with love. "Honey, you're perfect just the way you are. Even in your bathrobe with a towel around your head."

She giggled. "Be that as it may, a little paint never hurt any old barn. And I'm not going to get married in my bathrobe with a towel around my head."

He harrumphed. "I should hope not with what that wedding dress set me back."

His wife slapped him playfully on the shoulder. "Don't you start. You're the one who insisted on buying that dress."

"Then I want to see my daughter wearing it—which she won't be doing if she doesn't get a move on."

Kendra gave him a little shove out of the room. "So let me get dressed already."

An hour later, they had assembled at the church. Kendra had taken the precaution of bringing her dress to the church rather than wearing it in case of inclement weather. Now she sat in her wedding gown in front of the mirror as Molly applied the curling iron to her stubborn curls in an effort to tame them.

"It's no use, Molly," Kendra said with a laugh. "My hair is what it is. It's always had a mind of its own."

"It's okay. I love a challenge." Molly looked beautiful in her wine-colored, velvet bridesmaid's dress.

"I predict you're next," Kendra told her.

Molly waved her hand dismissively. "Not at the rate Tim is moving. The man has no clue."

Kendra studied her friend's reflection in the mirror. Although Molly's face bore a grin, Kendra detected a trace of frustration in her tone. "Molly, I have never known you to be one to beat around the bush. It's the twenty-first century, for heaven's sake. Propose to *him*!"

Molly sucked in her lips. "I can't. I'm old-fashioned that way."

"Then I suppose some of Tim's friends may have to give him a little nudge," Kendra said with a wink.

"Enough about me. I've done all I can with your hair." Molly unplugged the curling iron and set it on the dressing table.

"Thanks, Molly." Kendra stood and examined herself from different angles. "You worked wonders. But back to what we were just talking about. I'll aim the bridal bouquet at you. Maybe that will give Tim the hint."

Molly laughed. "Sounds good. I'll do my best to catch it even if I have to knock three other women out of the way."

The door opened, and Darcy and Audrey stepped into the room.

"You look stunning," said Darcy.

Kendra felt the heat of a blush on her face. "You all look lovely, too. Thank you so much for being my bridesmaids."

The door opened again, and Tania, her maid-of-honor joined them. "They're almost ready. We'd better get out there before the ring bearer and the flower girl get into a knock-down, drag-out fight."

Kendra's niece and nephew were doing the honors under protest. She sighed. "Do I have to do everything? Tell that brother of mine to make his little rug-rats behave or I'll give them all the icing flowers on the wedding cake, and he can deal with his sugar-amped kids for the rest of the day."

As they lined up for the processional, Kendra's heart overflowed with joy to the point she didn't think she could bear any more happiness. She stole a glimpse of Ricky standing by the altar looking simultaneously debonaire in his tux and decidedly out of his element without his boots and cowboy hat.

Whispering, "Thank you, God," she took her father's arm and waited as everyone marched down the aisle. When the organ music swelled to *The Bridal Chorus*, her heart did a little leap. This was it! Her nerves suddenly a jitter, she glanced around at the nearly full church, all eyes focused on her. How would she ever make it down that long aisle? Her throat constricted and her palms broke out in a sweat.

"Sweetheart?" Her father shot her a worried look and gave her a little tug into the sanctuary.

She swallowed and took a step forward. Then, catching Ricky's shining eyes on her, all her surroundings faded into the background as she zoned in on his face. Holding her head high, she marched the rest of the way until she stood next to him, ready to embark on their future together.

The ceremony passed in a blur, and before she knew it, the minister had pronounced them husband and wife. Ricky leaned in for a long kiss that drew an appreciative whoop from the audience and caused her face to flame. Then they turned and made their way back down the aisle behind the bridal party as everyone cheered.

Just as they reached the receiving line, she tripped on the hem of her long gown and went tumbling toward the floor. A gasp went up from the crowd, but Ricky caught her in his strong arms and set her upright.

"Good catch, Ricky!" came a voice from the crowd, as people started clapping.

Ricky looked at the group of well-wishers. "Yeah, she sure is." Turning to her, he whispered in her ear, "Red, you fell for me the first day we met. I'm glad to see you're still falling for me."

"Always, cowboy, always." She grinned at him and shoved a mass of curls from her face.

"That's *Professor Cowboy* if you don't mind."

"I don't mind," she said, throwing her arms around his neck and planting a kiss on his lips.

"Red!" he pulled away in mock shock. "People are watching."

"Tough. Let them get their own professor

cowboy." She winked at him and turned to greet the first people in the receiving line.

THANK YOU, DEAR READER

If you enjoyed reading this book, the best thing you can do to help the author is to tell others about it. Ellen would also greatly appreciate you rating her book and leaving a brief review at amazon.com and goodreads.com. Simply type in the name of the book and the author. When the website comes up, click on the picture of the book, scroll down, and there will be a button to click to leave a rating and a review. A review doesn't have to be long—a sentence or two telling what you liked about the book. Was it interesting, humorous, informative, thought-provoking, etc.? Thank you so much for your support.

Ellen would love for you to visit her website: https://ellenfannonauthor.com and subscribe to follow her weekly blog, *Good for a Laugh.*
Follow Ellen on Facebook:
https://www.facebook.com/ellenfannonauthor

SAVE THE DATE

2022 Christian Indie Award Winner

What if you were given the chance to rekindle the flame with your first love? What happened to all those girls who were mean to you in school? Should Hannah Jensen take the chance of attending her high school reunion to find out?

Hannah hasn't been back to her hometown in twenty-five years. Now a widow raising a teenaged daughter, she has the opportunity to go home for her twenty-fifth high school reunion. The invitation to the reunion stirs up a lot of old memories at the same time she is dealing with loneliness, the challenges of single-parenting a teenager, people who want to "set her up" with eligible men, her own insecurities, and her eccentric family.

The story interweaves the present with scenes from Hannah's past and her fantasy of "happily ever after" with her high school boyfriend in a humorous and entertaining manner. Her feelings from being "shunned" by the cool kids resurface as she reflects back on her time as a teenager. There are several roadblocks on Hannah's journey from a teenager through her present. The growing pains and amusing situations in which she finds herself are ones to which we all can relate. As she walks the path of self-discovery, she also discovers the most important life lesson of all–her relationship to God.

DON'T BITE THE DOCTOR

Real doctors treat more than one species. At least that's what veterinarian, Jill Bennet tells herself. On any given day, she may find herself doctoring dogs, cats, bunnies, birds, horses, pigs, or any other furry or feathered patient who crosses her path—striving daily to deliver compassion and competence to all God's creatures, in accordance with Colossians 3:23. Now, with over forty years of practice under her belt, Jill reflects back to her time as a new, young veterinarian in the early eighties—a time when women veterinarians were just beginning to become a presence among the previously male-dominated profession. Out in the real world, Jill finds herself in situations never covered in veterinary school. It is a journey of learning and laughter, as Jill contends with a variety of animal patients and their eclectic humans attached to the other end of the leash (and the checkbook), as well as less-than-helpful co-workers. Interwoven into this mix of new experiences is her budding romance with the owner of the sock-eating Labrador Retriever. *Don't Bite the Doctor* promises to bring smiles and tears to anyone who has ever been owned by an animal.

OTHER PEOPLE's CHILDREN

As a mid-thirties childless woman, Robin has all the answers on proper parenting. It doesn't take long, however, for Robin to realize that her perfect parenting ideas and reality often collide – the result being an amusing journey of finding out that God, indeed, has a sense of humor. As she deals with the baggage, idiosyncrasies, unique personalities, and special gifts of each child that crosses her path, she finds that there is no "one-size fits all" to parenting. However, in spite of the challenges she and her husband face, they are determined to become the children's strongest advocates in a flawed system that often fails the very victims it is designed to protect. The journey is often heartbreaking and frustrating, but these foster parents are firmly resolved that for whatever time they have children in their care, the children will know they are safe, protected, and loved by God, as well as by their foster parents.

HONOR THY FATHER
EPISODE ONE
HONOR THY FATHER
EPISODE TWO

Why should Adam's daughters, with whom he hasn't had contact for twenty-five years, honor him now when he needs a life-saving bone marrow transplant? Why should his son, who was kicked out of the house, honor his father? Is there any hope of reconciliation when twenty-five years of anger, bitterness, and divergent pathways have led family members down different roads of life? *Honor Thy Father* is the compelling story of loss and redemption and how God can turn tragedy into triumph.

How does a family survive after being torn apart? Adam Wallace copes with the heartbreaking loss of his wife and daughters by immersing himself in his work.

Charlotte withdraws from everyone and everything around her. Dana, living a life of privilege, does not even realize her loss. Katrina copes by trying to make everyone else happy. Scott copes by rebellion. Ultimately, they all come to realize that God can work through every situation to make beauty out of ashes.

LOVE IN THE WIND

Wyoming rancher, Ben Parish, is struggling to keep his ranch afloat. Veterinarian, Darcy Fuller has moved to Wyoming to start a new life but is struggling to become established in a new area. Both have been badly burned by past relationships and are not looking to become involved in another. When their paths cross, Darcy has an idea to bring extra income to the ranch, as well as provide her with an outlet for her passion for working with horses. But can their growing attraction coexist with a business partnership?